SAVED BY DOCTOR DREAMY

BY
DIANNE DRAKE

First published in Great Britain 2017
By Mills & Boon, an imprint of HarperCollins*Publishers*
1 London Bridge Street, London, SE1 9GF

Large Print edition 2017

ISBN: 978-0-263-06740-8

MIX
Paper from responsible sources
FSC™ C007454

This book is produced from independently certified FSC paper to ensure responsible forest management. For more information visit www.harpercollins.co.uk/green.

Printed and bound in Great Britain
by CPI Group (UK) Ltd, Croydon, CR0 4YY

Starting with non-fiction, **Dianne Drake** penned hundreds of articles and seven books under the name JJ Despain. In 2001 she began her romance-writing career with *The Doctor Dilemma*. In 2005 Dianne's first Medical Romance, *Nurse in Recovery*, was published, and with more than 20 novels to her credit she has enjoyed writing ever since.

Books by Dianne Drake

Mills & Boon Medical Romance

Deep South Docs

A Home for the Hot-Shot Doc
A Doctor's Confession

A Child to Heal Their Hearts
Tortured by Her Touch
Doctor, Mummy...Wife?
The Nurse and the Single Dad

Visit the Author Profile page
at millsandboon.co.uk for more titles.

Praise for
Dianne Drake

'A very emotional, heart-tugging story. A beautifully written book. This story brought tears to my eyes in several parts.'

—*Goodreads* on
P.S. You're a Daddy!

CHAPTER ONE

THE NIGHT WAS STILL. No howler monkeys sitting up in the trees yelling their heads off. No loud birds calling into the darkness. Damien doubted if there was even a panther on the prowl anywhere near here. It was kind of eerie actually, since he was used to the noise. First, the city noise in Seattle, where he grew up. Then Chicago, Miami, New York. Back to Seattle. And finally, the noise of the Costa Rican jungle, where he'd come to settle.

Noise was his friend. It comforted him, reassured him that he was still alive. Something he hadn't felt in a long, long time. And when it surrounded him, it was home and safety and all the things that kept him sane and focused on the life he was living now.

When Damien had come to the jungle he'd been pleasantly surprised by the noisiness of it all. It was as loud as any city, but in a different way. He'd traded in people for animals and honking cars for wind rustling through the vegetation. Now that he was used to the sounds there, he counted on them to surround him, to cradle him in a contented solitude. But tonight was different. He felt so…isolated, so out of touch with his reality. So lonely. Alone in the city—alone in the jungle. It was all the same. All of it bringing a sense of despair that caught up with him from time to time.

This despair of his had been a problem over the years. People didn't understand it. Didn't want to. Most of the time he didn't want to understand it either, because when he did he'd overcompensate. Do things he might not normally do. Like getting engaged to someone he wouldn't have normally given a second thought to.

But Daniel understood this about him. Daniel—he was the only one, and he'd never ridiculed Damien for what other people thought was ridiculous. Of course, he and Daniel had the twin-connection thing going on, and that was something that never failed him.

Damien and Daniel Caldwell. Two of a kind—well, not so much. They looked alike, with a few notable exceptions like hair length and beard. Daniel was the clean-shaven, short-haired version, while Damien was the long-haired, scruffy-bearded one. But they were both six foot one, had the same brown eyes, same dimples that women seemed to adore. Same general build. Apart from their outward looks, though, they couldn't have been more different. Restlessness and the need to keep moving were Damien's trademarks while contented domesticity and a quiet lifestyle were his brother's. Which Damien envied, as he'd always figured that by the time he was thirty-five he'd have something in his life more stable than what he had. Something substantial. Yet that hadn't happened.

It's too quiet tonight, Damien scribbled into a short letter to his brother. *It feels like it's going to eat me alive.* He'd seen Daniel a few months ago. Gone back to the States for Daniel's wedding. And it was a happy reunion, not like the time before that when he'd been called home to support his brother through his first wife's death. But Daniel had moved on now. He had a happy life, a happy family. Lucky, *lucky* man.

The work is good, though, bro. It keeps me busy pretty much all the time. Keeps me out of trouble. So how's your new life fitting into your work schedule?

Daniel's life—a nice dream. Even though, deep down, Damien didn't want strings to bind him to one place, one lifestyle. Rather, he needed to do what he wanted, when he wanted, with no one to account to. And space to think, to reevaluate. Or was that another of his overcompensations? Anyway, he had that now, although he'd had to come to the remote jungles of Costa Rica to find it. In that remoteness, however, he'd found a freedom he'd never really had before.

And remote it was. Isolated from all the everyday conveniences that Costa Rica's large cities offered. Not even attractive to the never-ending flow of expats who were discovering the charms of this newly modernizing Central American country.

Most of the time Damien thrived on the isolation, not that he was, by nature, a solitary kind of man. Because he wasn't. Or at least didn't used to be. In his former life, he'd liked fast cars, nice condos and beautiful women. In fact, he'd thrived on those things before he'd escaped them. Now, the lure of the jungle had trapped him in a self-imposed celibacy, and that wasn't just of a sexual nature. It was a celibacy from worldly matters. A total abstinence from anything that wasn't directed specifically toward him. A time to figure out where he was going next in his life. Or if he was even going to go anywhere else at all.

In the meantime, Damien didn't regret turning his back on his old life in order to take off on this new one. In ways he'd never expected, it suited him.

Say hello to Zoey for me, and tell her I'm glad she joined the family. And give Maddie a kiss from her Uncle Damien.

Damien scrawled his initials at the bottom of the letter, stuck it in an envelope and addressed it. Maybe sometime in the next week or so he'd head into Cima de la Montaña to stock up on some basic necessities and mail the letter. Call his parents if he got near enough to a cell tower. And find a damned hamburger!

"We need you back in the hospital, Doctor,"

Alegria Diaz called through his open window. She was his only trained nurse—a woman who'd left the jungle to seek a higher education. Which, in these parts, was a rarity as the people here didn't usually venture too far out into the world.

"What is it?" he called back, bending down to pull on his boots.

"Stomachache. Nothing serious. But he wouldn't listen to me. Said he had to see *el médico*."

El médico. The doctor. Yes, that was him. The doctor who directed one trained nurse, one semi-retired, burned-out plastic surgeon and a handful of willing, if not experienced, volunteers.

"Let me put my shirt back on and comb my hair, and I'll be right over." A year ago his world had been very large. Penthouse. Sports car. Today it was very small. A one-room hut twenty paces from the hospital. A borrowed pickup truck that worked as often as it didn't.

Damien donned a cotton T-shirt, pulled his hair back and rubber-banded it into a small pony-tail, and headed out the door. Being on call 24/7 wasn't necessarily the best schedule, but that was the life he'd accepted for himself and it was also the life he was determined to stick with. For how long? At least until he figured out what his next life would be. Or if he'd finally stumbled upon the life he wanted.

"I wanted to give him an antacid," Alegria told him as he entered through the door of El Hospital Bombacopsis, which sat central in the tiny village of Bombacopsis.

"But he refused it?" Damien asked, stopping just inside the door.

"He said a *resbaladera* would fix him."

Resbaladera—a rice and barley drink. "Well, we don't serve that here and, even if we did, I've never heard that it has any medicinal benefits for a stomachache."

Alegria smiled up at him. She was a petite woman, small in frame, short in height. Dark skin, black hair, dark eyes. Mother of three, grandmother of one. "He won't take an antacid from you," she warned.

"And yesterday he wouldn't take an aspirin from me when he had a headache. So why's he here in the first place, if he refuses medical treatment?"

"Señor Segura takes sick twice a year, when his wife goes off to San José to visit her sister."

"She leaves, and he catches a cold and comes to the hospital." Damien chuckled.

"Rosalita is a good cook here. He likes her food."

"Well, apparently he ate too much of it tonight, since he's sick at his stomach."

Alegria shrugged. "He's hard to control once you put a plate of *casado* in front of him."

Casado—rice, black beans, plantains, salad, tortillas and meat. One of Damien's favorite Costa Rican meals. But he didn't go all glutton on it the way Señor Segura apparently had. "Well, *casado* or not, I'm going to check him out, and if this turns out to be a simple stomachache from overeating I'm going to give him an antacid and tell Rosalita to cut back on his portions."

"He won't like that," Alegria said.

"And I don't like having my evening interrupted by a patient who refuses to do what his nurse tells him."

"Whatever you say, Doctor." Alegria scooted off to fetch the antacid while Damien approached his cantankerous patient.

"I hear you won't take the medicine my nurse wanted to give you."

"It's no good," Señor Segura said. "Won't cure what's wrong with me."

"But a rice and barley drink will?"

"That's what my Guadalupe always gives me when I don't feel so well."

"Well, Guadalupe is visiting her sister now, which means we're the ones who are going to have to make you feel better." Damien bent down and prodded the man's belly, then had a listen to his belly sounds through a stethoscope. He checked the chart for the vital signs Alegria had already recorded, then took a look down Señor Segura's throat. Nothing struck him as serious so he signaled Alegria to bring the antacid over to the bedside. "OK, you're sick. But it's only because you ate too much. My nurse is going to give you a couple of tablets to chew that will make you feel better."

"The tablets are no good. I want *resbaladera* like my Guadalupe makes."

Damien refused to let this man try his patience, which was going to happen very quickly if he didn't get this situation resolved. It was a simple matter, though. Two antacid tablets would work wonders, if he could convince Señor Segura to give in. "I don't have *resbaladera* here, and we're not going to make it specifically for you." They had neither the means nor the money to make special accommodations for one patient.

"Then I'll stay sick until I get better, or die!"

"You're not going to die from a stomachache," Damien reassured him.

"And I'm not going to die because I wouldn't take your pills."

So there it was. The standoff. It happened sometimes, when the village folk here insisted on sticking to their traditional ways. He didn't particularly like giving in, when he knew that what he was trying to prescribe would help. But in cases like Señor Segura's, where the cure didn't much matter one way or another, he found it easier to concede the battle and save his arguments for something more important.

"Well, if you're refusing the tablets, that's up to you. But just keep in mind that your stomachache could last through the night."

"Then let it," Señor Segura said belligerently. Then he looked over at Alegria. "And you can save those pills for somebody else."

Alegria looked to Damien for instruction. "Put them back," Damien told her.

"Yes, Doctor," she said, frowning at Señor Segura. "As you wish."

What he wished was that he had more space, better equipment, more trained staff and up-to-date medicines. In reality, though, he had a wood-frame, ten-bed hospital that afforded no luxuries whatsoever and a one-room, no-frills clinic just off the entrance to the ward. It was an austere setup, and he had to do the best with it that he could. But the facility's lack was turning into his lack of proper service, as he didn't have much to offer anyone. Basic needs were about all he could meet. Of course, it was his choice to trade in a lucrative general surgery practice in Seattle for all of this. So he wasn't complaining. More like, he was wishing.

One day, he thought to himself as he took a quick look at the only other patient currently admitted to the hospital. She was a young girl with a broken leg whose parents couldn't look after her properly and still tend to their other nine children. So he'd set her leg, then admitted her, and wasn't exactly sure what to do with her other than let her occupy space until someone more critical needed the bed.

"She's fine," Alegria told him before he took his place at the bedside. "I checked her an hour ago and she's sound asleep."

Damien nodded and smiled. The only thing that would turn this worthless evening into something worthwhile would be to shut himself in his clinic and take a nap on the exam table. Sure, it was the lazy way out, since his real bed was only a few steps away. But his exam room was closer, and he was suddenly bone-tired. And his exam table came with a certain appeal he couldn't, at this moment, deny. So Damien veered off to the clinic, shut the door behind him and was almost asleep before he stretched out on the exam room table.

"Like I've been telling you for the past several weeks, I don't want a position in administration here at your hospital. I don't want to be your side-kick. I don't want to be put through the daily grind of budgets and salaries and supply orders!"

Juliette Allen took a seat across the massive mahogany desk from her father, Alexander, and leaned forward. "And, most of all, I don't want to be involved in anything that smacks of nepotism." Standing up to her dad was something she should have done years ago, but first her schooling, then her work had overtaken her, thrown her into a rut. Made her complacent. Then one day she woke up in the same bedroom she'd spent thirty-three years waking up in, had breakfast at the same table she'd always had breakfast at, and walked out the front door she'd always walked out of. Suddenly, she'd felt stifled. Felt the habits of her life closing in around her, choking her. And that's what her life had turned into—one big habit.

"This isn't nepotism, Juliette," Alexander said patiently. "It's about me promoting the most qualified person to the position."

"But I didn't apply for the position!" She was too young to be a director of medical operations in a large hospital. The person filling that spot needed years more experience than she had and she knew that. What she also knew was that this was her father's way of keeping her under his thumb. "And I think it's presumptuous of you to submit an application on my behalf."

"You're qualified, Juliette. And you have a very promising future."

"I direct the family care clinic, another position you arranged for me."

"And your clinic is one of the best operated in this hospital." Dr. Alexander Allen was a large man, formidable in his appearance, very sharp, very direct. "This is a good opportunity for you, and I don't understand why you're resisting me."

"Because I haven't paid my dues, because I don't have enough experience to direct the medical workings of an entire hospital." The problem was, she'd always given in to her father. Juliette's mother had died giving birth to her, and he'd never remarried, so it had always been just the two of them, which made it easy for him to control her with guilt over causing her mother's death. Plus she was also consumed by the guilt of knowing that if she left him he wouldn't fare so well on his own. For all his intelligence and power in the medical world, her father was insecure in his private world. Juliette's mother had done *everything* for him, then it fell to Juliette to do the same.

Juliette adored her dad, despite the position

he'd put her in. He'd been a very good father to her, always making sure she had everything she wanted and needed. *More* than she wanted and needed, actually. And she'd become accustomed to that opulent lifestyle, loved everything about it, which was why this was so difficult now. She was tied to the man in a way most thirty-three-year-old women were not tied to their fathers. Which was why her dad found it so easy to make his demands then sit back and watch her comply.

"I just can't do this, Dad," she said, finally sitting back in her chair. "And I hope you can respect my position."

"You're seriously in jeopardy of missing your opportunity to promote yourself out of your current job, Juliette. When I was a young man, in a situation much like the one you're in, I was always the first person in line to apply for any position that would further my career."

"But you've always told me that your ultimate career goal was to do what you're doing now—run an entire hospital. You, yourself, said you weren't cut out for everyday patient care."

"And my drive to get ahead has provided you with a good life. Don't you forget that."

"I'm not denying it, Dad. I appreciate all you've done for me and I love the life you've given me. But it's time for me to guide my career without your help." Something she should have done the day she'd entered medical school, except she hadn't even broken away from him then. She'd stayed at home, gone to the university and medical school where her father taught because it was easier for him. And while that wasn't necessarily her first choice, she always succumbed to her father when he started his argument with: "Your mother died giving birth to you and you can't even begin to understand how rough that's been on me, trying to take care of you, trying to be a good father—"

It was the argument he'd used time and time again when he thought he was about to lose her, the one that made her feel guilty, the one that always caused her to cave. But not this time. She'd made the decision first, then acted on it before she told him. And *this* time she was resolved to break away, because if she didn't she'd end up living the life he lived. Alone. Substituting work for a real life.

"And it's not about going into an administrative position, Dad." Now she had to drop the *real* bomb, and it wasn't going to be easy. "In fact, I have something somewhat administrative in mind for what I want to do next."

"Why do I have a feeling that what you're about to tell me is something I'm not going to like?" He looked straight across at his daughter. "I'm right, am I not?"

Juliette squared all five foot six of herself in her chair and looked straight back at him. "You're right. And there's no easy way to put this." She stopped, waiting for him to say something, but when he didn't she continued. "I'm going to resign from my position here at the hospital, Dad. In fact, I'm going to turn in my one-month notice tomorrow and have a talk with Personnel on how to replace me."

"You're leaving," he stated. "Just turning your back on everything you've accomplished here and walking out the door."

"I'm not turning my back on it, and I may come back someday. But right now, I've got to do something on my own, something you didn't just hand me. And whether you want to admit it or not, all my promotions have been gifts. I didn't earn them the way I should have."

"But you've worked hard in every position you've had, and you've shown very good judgment and skill in everything you've done."

"A lot of doctors can do that, Dad. I just happened to be the one whose father was Chief of Staff."

"So you're quitting because I'm Chief of Staff?"

"No, I'm quitting because I'm the chief of staff's daughter."

"Have I really piled that many unrealistic expectations on you? Because if I have, I can back off."

"It's not about backing off. It's about letting go." She didn't want to hurt him, but he did have to understand that it was time for her to spread her wings. Test new waters. Take a different path. "I— *We* have to do it. It's time."

"But can't you let go and still work here?"

"No." She shut her eyes for a moment, bracing herself for the rest of this. "I've accepted another position."

"Another hospital? There aren't any better hospitals in Indianapolis than Memorial."

"It's not a hospital, and it's not in Indianapolis." She swallowed hard. "I'm going to Costa Rica."

"The hell you are!" he bellowed. "What are you thinking, Juliette?"

She knew this was hard on him, and she'd considered leading up to this little by little. But her dad was hardheaded, and he was as apt to shut out the hints she might drop as he was to listen to them. Quite honestly, Alexander Allen heard only what he wanted to hear.

"What I'm thinking is that I've already made arrangements for a place to stay, and I'll be leaving one month from Friday."

"To do what?"

Now, this was where it became even more difficult. "I'm going to head up a medical recruitment agency."

Her dad opened up his mouth to respond, but shut it again when nothing came out.

"The goal is to find first-rate medical personnel to bring there. Costa Rica, and even Central America as a whole, can't supply the existing demand for medical professionals so they're recruiting from universities and hospitals all over the world, and I'm going to be in charge of United States recruitment."

"I know about medical recruitment. Lost a top-rate radiologist to Thailand a couple of years ago."

"So you know how important it is to put the best people in situations where they can help a hospital or, in Costa Rica's case, provide the best quality of care they can to the greatest number of people."

"Which leaves people like me in the position of having to find a new radiologist or transplant surgeon or oncologist, depending on who you're recruiting away from me."

"But you're already in an easier position to find the best doctors to fill your positions. You have easier access to the medical schools, a never-ending supply of residents to fill any number of positions in the hospital and you have connections to every major hospital in the country. These are things Costa Rica doesn't have, so in order for them to find the best qualified professionals they have to reach out differently than you do. Which, in this case, will be through me."

It was an exciting new venture for her and, while she wouldn't be offering direct medical care herself, she envisioned herself involved in a great, beneficial service. And all she ever wanted to be as a doctor was someone who benefited her patients, and by providing the patients in Costa Rica with good health-care practitioners she'd be helping more patients than she'd ever be able to help as a single practitioner in a clinic. In fact, when she thought about how many lives only one single recruited doctor could improve, she was overwhelmed. And when she thought of how many practitioners she would recruit and how many patients they would touch, it boggled her mind. "It's an important job, Dad. And I'm excited about it."

"Excited or not, you're throwing away a good medical career. You were a fine *hospital* physician, Juliette. In whatever capacity you chose."

"You were, too, once upon a time, but you traded that in for a desk and thousand-dollar business suits. So don't just sit there and accuse me of leaving medicine, because I'm not doing anything that you haven't already done."

"But in Costa Rica? Why there? Why not investigate something *different* closer to home, if you're hell-bent on getting out of Memorial. Maybe medical research. We've got one of the world's largest facilities just a few miles from here. Or maybe teaching. I mean, we've got, arguably, one of the best medical schools in the country right at our back door."

"But I don't want to teach, and I especially don't want to do research. I also don't want to work for an insurance company or provide medical care for a national sports franchise. What I want, Dad, is to find something that excites me. Something that offers a large group of people medical services they might not otherwise get. Something that will help an entire country improve its standard of care."

"There's nothing I can do to change your mind?" her dad asked, sounding as if the wind had finally been knocked out of his sails.

Juliette shook her head. "No, Dad. There's not. I've been looking into the details of my new position for weeks now, and I'm truly convinced this is something I want to do at this point in my life."

"Well, I'm going to leave your position open for a while. Staff it with a temp, in case you get to Costa Rica and decide your new job isn't for you. That way, you'll have a place to come back to, just in case."

Her dad was a handsome, vital man, and she hoped that once she was gone, and he didn't have anybody else to depend on, he might actually go out and get a life for himself. Maybe get married. Or travel. Or sail around the world the way he used to talk about when she was a little girl. In some ways, Juliette felt as if she'd been holding him back. She still lived with him, worked with him, was someone to keep him company when no one else was around. It was an easy way for both of them but she believed that so much togetherness had stunted them both. She didn't date, hadn't dated very much as a whole, thanks to her work commitments, and she'd certainly never gone out and looked for employment outside of what her father had handed her.

Yes, that was all easy. But now it was over. It was time for her to move on. "If I do come back to Indianapolis in the future, I won't be coming back to Memorial because I don't think it's a good idea that we work together anymore. We need to be separate, and if I'm here at Memorial that's not going to happen."

"Is this about something I've done to you,

Juliette?" he asked, sounding like a totally defeated man.

"No, Dad. It's about something I haven't done for myself." And about everything she wanted to do for herself in the future.

One month down, and so far she was enjoying her new job. She'd had the opportunity to interview sixteen potential candidates for open positions in various hospitals. Seven doctors, three registered nurses, three respiratory therapists, a physical therapist and two X-ray technicians, one of whom specialized in mammograms. And there were another ten on her list for the upcoming two weeks. The bonus was, she loved Costa Rica. What she'd seen of it so far was beautiful. The people were nice. The food good. The only thing was, her lifestyle was a bit more subdued than what she was used to. She didn't have a nice shiny Jaguar to drive, but a tiny, used compact car provided by the agency. And her flat—not exactly luxurious like her home back in Indiana, but she was getting used to smaller, no-frills quarters and cheaper furniture. It was a drastic lifestyle change, she did have to admit, but she was doing the best she could with what she had.

Perhaps the most drastic change, though—the one thing she hadn't counted on—was that she missed direct patient care in a big way. She'd reconciled herself to experiencing some withdrawal before she'd come here, but what she'd been feeling was overwhelming as she'd never considered that stepping away from it would take such an emotional toll on her. But it had. She was restless. When she didn't stop herself, her mind wandered back to the days when she'd been involved directly in patient care. And it wasn't that she didn't like her job, because she did, and she had no intention of walking away from it. But she could physically, as well as emotionally, feel the lack in herself and she was afraid it was something that was only going to continue growing if she didn't find a fix for it.

"Are you sure you want to go through with this?" Cynthia Jurgensen, her office mate as well as her roommate, asked her. Like Juliette, Cynthia was a medical recruiter. Her recruitment area was the Scandinavian countries, as she had a heritage there. And, like Juliette, Cynthia had experienced the thrill of being called to a new adventure.

"Well, the note I found posted on the internet says the scheduling is flexible, so I'm hoping to work it out that I can commute in Friday night after I leave work here, and come home either late Sunday night or early Monday morning, before I'm due back on this job."

"But it's in the jungle, Juliette. The jungle!"

"And it's going to allow me to be involved with direct patient care again. I'm just hoping it's enough to satisfy me."

"Well, you can do whatever you want, but leave me here in the city, with all my conveniences."

San José was a large city, not unlike any large city anywhere. Juliette's transition here had been minimal as she really hadn't had time to get out and explore much of anything. So maybe her first real venture out, into the jungle of all places, was a bit more than most people would like, but the only thing Juliette could see was an opportunity to be a practicing doctor again. A doctor by the name of Damien Caldwell had advertised and, come tomorrow, she was going to go knocking on his door.

* * *

"Could you get one of the volunteers to take the linens home and wash them?" Damien asked Alegria. The hospital's sheets and pillowcases were a motley assortment, most everything coming as donations from the locals. "Oh, and instruct Rosalita on the particulars of a mechanical diet. I'm admitting Hector Araya later on, and he has difficulty chewing and swallowing since he had his stroke, so we need to adjust his diet accordingly."

Back in Seattle, Damien's workload never came close to anything having to do with linens and food but here in Bombacopsis, everything in the hospital fell under his direct supervision. This morning, for instance, during his one and only break for the day, he'd even found himself fluffing pillows and passing out cups of water to the five patients now admitted. He didn't mind the extra work, actually. It was just all a part of the job here. But he wondered if having another trained medical staffer come in, at least part-time, would ease some of the burden. That was why, when he'd gone to Cima de la Montaña last week to mail his letter to Daniel, he'd found a computer and posted a help-wanted ad on one of the local public sites.

Low pay, or possibly no pay.
Lousy hours and hard work.
Nice patients desperately in need of more medical help.

That was all his ad said, other than where to find him. *No phone service. Come in person.*

OK, so it might not have been the most appealing of ads. But it was honest, as the last thing he wanted was to have someone make that long trek into the jungle only to discover that their expectations fell nowhere within the scope of the position he was offering.

"There's a woman outside who says she wants to see you," Alegria said as she rushed by him, her arms full of bedsheets, on her way to change the five beds with patients in them.

"Can't one of the volunteers do that for you?" Damien asked her. "Or Dr. Perkins?"

"Dr. Perkins is off on a house call right now, and I have only two volunteers on today. One is cleaning the clinic, and the other is scrubbing potatoes for dinner. So it's either you or me and, since the woman outside looks determined to get in, I think I'll change the sheets and leave that woman up to you."

"Fine," Damien said, setting aside the chart he'd been writing in. "I'll go see what she wants. Is she a local, by the way?"

Alegria shook her head. "She's one of yours."

"Mine?"

"From the United States, I think. Or maybe Canada. Couldn't tell from her accent."

So a woman, possibly from North America somewhere, had braved the jungle to come calling. At first he wondered if she was some kind of pharmaceutical rep who'd seen the word *hospital* attached to this place and actually thought she might find a sale here. As if he had the budget to go after the newest, and always the most expensive, drugs. *Nah.* He was totally off the radar for that. So, could it be Nancy? Was she running after him, trying to convince him to give up his frugal ways and come back to her?

Been there, done that one. Found out he couldn't tolerate the snobs. And if there ever was a snob, it was his ex-fiancée.

"I'm Juliette Allen," the voice behind him announced.

Damien spun around and encountered the most stunning brown eyes he'd ever seen in his life. "I'm Damien Caldwell," he said, extending his hand to shake hers. "And I wasn't expecting you." But, whoever she was, he was glad she'd come. Tall, long auburn hair pulled back into a ponytail, ample curves, nice legs—nice everything. Yes, he was definitely glad.

"Your ad said to come in person, so here I am—in person."

In person, and in very good form, he thought. "Then you're applying for a position?" Frankly, she wasn't what he'd expected. Rather, he'd expected someone like George Perkins, a doctor who was in the middle of a career burnout, trying to figure out what to do with the rest of his life.

"Only part-time. I can give you my weekends, if you need me."

"Weekends are good. But what are you? I mean, am I hiring a nurse, a respiratory therapist or what?"

"A physician. I'm a family practice doctor. Directed a hospital practice back in Indiana."

"But you're here now, asking me for work?" From director of a hospital practice to this? It didn't make sense. "And you only want a couple days a week?"

"That's all I have free. The rest of my time goes to recruiting medical personnel to come to Costa Rica."

Now it was beginning to make some sense. She aided one of the country's fastest growing industries in her real life and wanted to be a do-gooder in her off time. Well, if the do-gooder had the skills, he'd take them for those two days. The rest of her time didn't matter to him in the least. "You can provide references?" he asked, not that he cared much to have a look at them, but the question seemed like the right one to ask.

"Whatever you need to see."

"And you understand the conditions here? And the fact that I might not have enough money left over in my budget to pay you all the time—or ever?"

"It's not about the money."

Yep. She was definitely a do-gooder. "So what's it about, Juliette?"

"I like patient care, and I don't get to do that in

my current position. I guess you can say I'm just trying to get back to where I started."

Well, that was as good a reason as any. And, in spite of himself, he liked her. Liked her no-nonsense attitude. "So, if I hire you, when can you start?"

"I'm here now, and I don't have to be back at my other job until Monday. I packed a bag, just in case I stayed, so I'm ready to work whenever you want me to start."

"How about now? I have some beds that need changing and a nurse who's doing that but who has other things to do. So, can you change a bed, Juliette?"

CHAPTER TWO

COULD SHE CHANGE a bed? Sad to say, she hadn't made very many beds in her life. Back home, she and her dad had a housekeeper who did that for them. Twice a week, fresh sheets on every bed in the house, whether or not the bed had been slept on. At her dad's insistence. Oh, and brand-new linens ordered from the finest catalogs once every few months.

That was her life then, all of it courtesy of a very generous and doting father, and she'd found nothing extraordinary about it as it had been everything she'd grown used to. Her dad had always told her it was his duty to spoil her, and she'd believed that. Now, today, living in San José, and in keeping with what she was accustomed to, she and Cynthia rented a flat that came with limited maid service. It cost them more to secure that particular amenity in their living quarters, but having someone else do the everyday chores was well worth the extra money. So, at thirty-three, Juliette was a novice at this, and pretty much every other domestic skill most people her age had long since acquired. But how difficult could it be to change a silly bed? She was smart, and capable. And if she could cure illnesses, she could surely slap a sheet onto the bed.

Easier said than done, Juliette discovered after she'd stripped the first bed, then laid a clean sheet on top of it. Tuck in the edges, fold under the corners, make sure there were no wrinkles—

She struggled through her mental procedural list, thought she was doing a fairly good job of it, all things considered. That was, until she noticed the sizable wrinkle that sprang up in the middle of the bed and crept all the way to the right side. How had that gotten there? she wondered as she tugged at the sheet from the opposite side, trying to smooth it out and, in effect, making the darned thing even worse.

"That could be uncomfortable, if you're the one who has to sleep on it," Damien commented from the end of the bed, where he was standing, arms folded across his chest, watching her struggle. "Causes creases in the skin if you lay on it too long."

"I intend to straighten it out. Maybe remake the bed." Actually, that was a lie. Her real intent was still to pat it down as much as she could, then move on to the next bed and hope the future occupant of this particular bed didn't have a problem with wrinkles.

"You know you've been working on this first bed for ten minutes now? Alegria would have had all five beds changed in that amount of time, and been halfway through giving a patient a bed bath. So what's holding you up? Because I have other things for you to do if you ever get done here."

"This is taking a little longer because I'm used to fitted sheets," she said defensively. Her response didn't make any sense, not to her, probably not to Damien, but it was the best she could come up with, other than the truth, which was that she just didn't do beds. How lame would that sound? Top-notch doctor felled by a simple bedsheet.

"Fitted sheets—nope, no such luxuries around here. In fact, our sheets are all donations from some of the locals. *Used* bedsheets, Juliette. The very best we have to offer. Rough-texture, well-worn hand-me-downs. But I'll bet you're used to a nice silk, or even an Egyptian cotton, maybe a fifteen-hundred thread count? You know, the very best the market has to offer."

Who would have guessed Damien knew sheets? But, apparently, he did. And, amazingly, what he'd described was exactly what she had on her bed back home. Nice, soft, dreadfully expensive sheets covering a huge Victorian, dark cherry-wood, four-poster antique of a bed. Her bed and sheets—luxuries she'd thought she couldn't live without until she'd come to Costa Rica, where such luxuries were scarce, and only for those who could afford to have them imported. Which her father would do for her, gladly, if she asked him. Although she'd never ask, as that would build up his hopes that she was already getting tired of her life in Costa Rica and wanted her old life back. Back home. Same as before. Returning to her old job. Taking the position as her father's chief administrative officer. Yes, that was the way his mind would run through it, all because she wanted better bedsheets.

OK, so she was a bit spoiled. She'd admit it

if anyone—Damien—cared to ask but, since he wasn't asking, she wasn't telling. Not a blessed thing! "The sheet you're describing would have cost a hundred and twenty times more than all the sheets in this ward put together. And that would be just one sheet."

"Ah! A lady with a passion for sheets." Damien arched mocking eyebrows. "I hope that same passion extends to your medicine."

"You mean a lady *doctor* who's being interrupted while she's trying to do her job." She regarded him for a moment. Well-muscled body. Three or four days' growth of stubble on his face. Over-the-collar hair, which he'd pulled back into a ponytail, not too unlike her own, only much, much shorter. Really nice dimples when he smiled. Sexy dimples. Kissable dimples… Juliette shook her head to clear the train wreck going on inside and went back to assessing her overall opinion of Damien Caldwell. He was stunningly handsome, which he probably knew, and probably used it to his advantage. Insufferably rude. Intelligent. Good doctor.

"Does it bother you that I'm watching?" he asked.

"What bothers me is that you think you know all about me through my bedsheets. You're judging me, aren't you? You know, poor little rich girl. Never changed a bedsheet in her life. That's what you're thinking, isn't it?" Judging her based on what she owned and not what she could do as a doctor.

"I wasn't but, now that you brought it up, I could. Especially if you *do* own Egyptian cotton."

"What I do or do not own has no bearing on the job here. And if you want to stand there speculating on something as unimportant as my sheets, be my guest. Speculate to your heart's content. But keep it to yourself because I need to get these beds changed and I *don't* need any distractions while I'm doing it."

The ad she'd read about this job should have warned her that it came with a pompous boss because he was, indeed, pompous. Full of himself. Someone who probably took delight in the struggles of others. "And in the meantime I'm going to smooth this stupid wrinkle so I can get on to the next bed."

"Well, if you ever get done here, I've got a patient coming into the clinic in a little while who has a possible case of gout in his left big toe. Could you take a look at him when he arrives?"

Gout. A painful inflammatory process, starting in the big toe in about half of all diagnosed cases. "I don't suppose we can test for hyperuricemia, can we?" Hyperuricemia was a build-up of uric acid in the blood. With elevated levels, its presence could precipitate an onset of gout.

"Nope. Haven't got the proper equipment to do much more than a simple CBC." Complete blood count. "And we do those sparingly because they cost us money we don't have."

"Then how do we diagnose him, or anybody else, for that matter, if we don't have the tests at our disposal?"

"The old-fashioned way. We apply common sense. In this particular case, you assess to see if it's swollen or red. You ask him if it hurts, then find out how and when. Also, you take into account the fact that the patient's a male, and we all know that men are more susceptible to gout than women. So that's another indicator. And the pain exists *only* in his big toe. Add it all up and you've got…gout." He took a big sweeping bow with his pronouncement, as if he was the lead character in a show on Broadway.

Juliette noticed his grand gesture, but chose to ignore it. "OK, it's gout. I'll probably agree with you once I've had a look at him. But, apart from that, what kind of drugs do you have on hand to treat him with? Nonsteroidal anti-inflammatories? Steroids? Colchicine? Maybe allopurinol?"

"Aspirin," he stated flatly.

"Aspirin? That's it?" Understaffed, understocked—what kind of place was this?

"We're limited here to the basics and that's pretty much how we have to conduct business every day. We start on the most simple level we can offer and hope that's good enough."

"What else do you have besides aspirin?"

"Antacids, penicillin, a lot of different topical ointments for bug bites, rashes and whatever else happens to a person's skin. A couple of different kinds of injectable anesthetic agents. Nitroglycerine. Cough syrup. Some antimicrobials. Antimalarials—mostly quinidine. A very small supply of codeine. Oh, and a handful of various other drugs that we can coerce from an occasional outsider who wanders through. When you have time, take a look. We keep the drugs in the locked closet just outside the clinic door."

"Are any of these expired drugs?"

"Hey, we take what we can get. So if it's not *too* expired, we accept it and, believe me, we're glad to get it. One person's expired drug may be another person's salvation."

"Isn't that dangerous?"

He shook his head. "I check with the pharmaceutical company before I use it. I mean, commercial expiration date is one thing, but some drugs have usable life left beyond their shelf life."

"But you do turn away some drugs that are expired?"

"Of course I do. I'm not going to put a patient at risk with an expired drug that's not usable."

"So when you call these pharmaceutical companies, don't they offer to stock you with new drugs?"

"All the time. But who the hell can afford *that* around here?" Damien shrugged. "Like I say, I check it to make sure it's safe, then I use it if it is, and thank my lucky stars I have it to use."

She hadn't expected anything lavish, but she also hadn't expected this much impoverishment.

Of course, she knew little clinics like this operated all over the world, barely keeping their doors open, scraping and bowing to get whatever they had. But, in her other life, those were only stories, not a real situation as it applied to her. Now, though, she was in the heart of make-do medicine and nothing in her education or experience had taught her how to get along within its confines.

"How do you learn to get by the way you do?" she asked Damien. "With all these limitations and hardships?"

He studied her for a moment, then smiled. "Most of it you simply make up as you go. I was a general surgeon in Seattle. Worked in one of the largest hospitals in the city—a teaching hospital. So I had residents and medical students at my disposal, every piece of modern equipment known to the medical world, my OR was second to none."

"And you gave it all up for this?" It was an admirable thing to do, but the question that plagued her about that was how anyone could go from so modern to so primitive? She'd done a little internet research on Damien before she'd come here, and he had a sterling reputation. He'd received all kinds of recognition for his achievements in surgery, and he'd won awards. So what made a person trade it for a handful of expired medicines and good guesses instead of proper tests and up-to-date drugs?

Maybe he had a father who ran the hospital, Juliette thought, as her own reasons for leaving her hospital practice crossed her mind.

"This isn't so bad once you get used to it," he said.

"But how do you get used to it? Especially when it's so completely different from your medical background?"

"You look at the people you're treating and understand that they need and deserve the best care you can give them, just the way that patients in any hospital anywhere else do. Only out here you're the only one to do it. I think that's the hardest part to get used to—the fact that there's no one else to fall back on. No equipment, no tests or drugs, no excuses…

"It scared me when I first got here until I came to terms with how I was going to have to rely on myself and all my skills and knowledge. That didn't make working in this hospital any easier, but it did put things into proper perspective."

"You've gotten used to it, haven't you?"

"Let's just say that I've learned to work with the knowledge that the best I can hope for is what I have on hand at the moment, and the people here who want medical help are grateful for whatever I have to offer. They don't take it for granted the way society in general has come to take much of its medical care for granted. So, once you understand that, you can get used to just about anything this type of practice will hand you."

"Then you don't really look forward, do you?"

"Can't afford to. If I did, I'd probably get really disappointed, because anything forward from this point is the same as anything looking backward. Nothing changes and, in practical terms, it probably never will."

"But you chose a jungle practice over what you had for some reason. Was it a conscious choice, or did you come here with expectation of one thing and get handed something else?"

"I got recruited to one of the leading hospitals by someone like you. They wanted my surgical skills and they came up with a pretty nice package to offer me. Since I've never stayed in any one position too long—"

"Why not?" she interrupted.

"Because there's always something else out there. Something I haven't tried yet. Something that might be better than what I've had." Something to distract him from the fact that he'd never found what he wanted.

"In other words, you're never contented?"

"In other words, I like to change up my life every now and then. Which is why I came here to Costa Rica. The country is recruiting doctors, the whole medical industry is competing in a worldwide arena and it sounded exciting. Probably like it did to you when they came calling on you. And I'm assuming they did come calling."

"Something like that." But her motive in coming here wasn't because she was restless, or that she simply needed a change in pace. Her acceptance came because she needed to expand herself in new directions. Someplace far, far away from her father.

"Well, anyway—they did a hard recruit on me. Kept coming back for about a year, until I finally decided to give it a shot."

"So you *did* work in one of the hospitals in San José?"

"For about a month. The timing was perfect. I'd just ended a personal relationship, which made me restless to go someplace, do something else. You know, running away. Which actually has been my habit for most of my adult life." Damien grinned. "Anyway, they offered, eventually I accepted, and it took me about a week to figure out I hated it."

"Why?"

"Because it was just like what I'd left. Brought back old memories of my last hospital, of how my former fiancée thought I should be more than a general surgeon, of how my future father-in-law said that being a general surgeon was so working class. Like there's something wrong with being working class! I'd always loved working for a living but that one criticism so totally changed me, there were times I didn't even recognize myself. Tried to be what my future family considered their equal. Put on airs I didn't have a right to. Drowned myself in a lifestyle that I didn't like, just to play the perfect part." He shook his head. "I really needed something different after I got through all that. Got it all sorted—who I *really* was, what I *really* wanted to do with my life. So one day I saw an ad where a little jungle hospital needed a doctor..."

"Like the ad you placed?" He had so much baggage in his past, she wondered how he'd gotten past it to reach this point in his life. It took a lot of strength to get from where he used to be to where he was now. A strength she wished she had for herself.

Damien chuckled. "The *same* ad."

"The *exact* same ad?" she asked him.

"One and the same. No pay, hard work, long hours. Nothing like I'd ever been involved with before. So, since I'd come to Costa Rica seeking a new adventure—hell, what's more of an adventure than this?"

"Maybe a hospital with Egyptian cotton sheets?" Everyone had something to run away from, she supposed. He did. She did. It was lucky for both of them that their need to run away had coincided with a place for them to go. Whether running into each other would turn out to be a good thing remained to be seen.

"I've lowered my expectations these past few months. If I have *any* bedsheets, I'm happy."

"But they didn't train you in medical school to be concerned about the sheets."

"And they didn't train *you* in medical school how to be a recruiter. Which makes me wonder if it's a good fit for you since you came knocking on my humble little door, wanting something different than what you already had. Ever think you made the wrong choice, that you belong back in your old life?"

OK, based on the little bit she knew about him, this was the Damien she'd expected. Not the one who almost garnered her admiration, but the one who annoyed her. "I made a very good choice coming to Costa Rica, regardless of what you think!" He was beginning to sound like her father. *Bad choice, Juliette. Think about it. You'll come to your senses.* "Not that it's any of your business."

"In my hospital, it *is* my business. Everything here is my business, including you. Because you working here affects everything else around you, and I have to protect the hospital's interests."

"What's your point?" she snapped.

"That's for you to figure out. Which, I'm sure, will happen in time."

"There's nothing to figure out. I accepted a position that brings first-rate medical professionals here. It's an honorable job and I like it. It's…important."

"I'm not saying that it's not. With the need to improve medical conditions expanding, I'm sure it's becoming a very important position. But is it important *enough* to you? Or is patient care more important?"

"Why can't both be important to me?"

"In my experience, I've found that we poor mortals don't always do a good job of dividing ourselves."

"That's assuming I'm divided."

"Well, I suppose only you know if that's the case." Damien stepped away from the bed. "Anyway, your patient will be here shortly, so I'd suggest you figure out some way to expedite those bedsheets so you can go be a *real* doctor." With that, he spun around and started walking away.

"Are you always so rude?" she asked him while he was still within earshot. He was not only rude, he was also nosy, presumptuous and out of line.

Damien stopped and turned back to face her. "I do it rather well, don't you think?"

Struggling with simple bedsheets, the way she was doing right now, was almost cute. It was painfully obvious, though, that this was a chore far beyond her capabilities. Or one she'd never before practiced. Which reminded Damien of days gone by, and one of the reasons he was here in the jungle, hiding away from civilization. Juliette was obviously a rich girl, probably out on her own in the world for the very first time and, once upon a time, he'd almost married a rich girl who probably still wasn't out in the world.

Spoiled was the word that always came to mind when he thought about Nancy. It was a word he wanted to apply to Juliette as well, but the determination he could see in her stopped him short of going that far. The fact was, Nancy would have never set foot in his jungle clinic and Juliette was here, fighting to make a difference. Which didn't exactly fit his perception of a rich girl.

OK, he had a bias. He admitted it. Hated that he'd just shown a bit of it to Juliette, by raising the doubt that she could cut it here. But it was well deserved, considering how he'd endured months of spoiled behavior from a woman he'd planned on marrying. Not that Nancy had ever played spoiled rich girl when it was just the two of them. No, she'd been sweet and attentive, convincing him she was the one to settle down for. Or in *Juliette's* case, *she* was the one he needed here to help him.

But in the end, Nancy had told him he could never be enough for her. He couldn't give her enough, as her demands had grown larger. More time. More attention. More of everything. He'd tried. He'd honestly tried. Bought her everything she wanted, which put him into deep debt. Cut back his hours at the hospital to spend more time with her, which almost cost him his job. No matter what he'd done, though, it hadn't been adequate. So he'd tried harder, and always failed.

As far as Juliette working here—could that be enough for her? Or was he overthinking this thing? Truth was, he was wary. With Nancy, the vicious circle he'd got himself trapped in had played against his self-esteem and it hadn't helped when her parents told him that he'd always be struggling, that he'd never have enough to give her what she deserved. Things. Lots and lots of material things. And social status. Even with his surgeon's salary and his position at the hospital, and all the awards he'd won, they were right. At least, he'd thought so at the time.

Anyway, she'd moved out of his apartment and gone home, straight into Mommy's and Daddy's arms. As far as he knew, two years later, she was still there, dwelling quite happily as their spoiled-rotten daughter. Probably waiting for Daddy to fix her up with a man who fit the family image. A man who could give her the things Damien could not.

Which, admittedly, stung. He'd reeled from the breakup for weeks, wondering what he could have done differently. Wondering why he'd thought he was good enough for Nancy when, obviously, he was not. Wondering why he'd chosen Nancy in the first place.

So, was Juliette that spoiled? Would she spend a day or an entire weekend here, only to discover that it wasn't enough for her? Would she walk away when she realized he couldn't give her proper bedsheets, let alone a proper bed? Bottom line—he needed her here. Recruits didn't come knocking every day when he advertised. And when they did show up, they usually turned right back around and left. In fact, other than George Perkins, she'd been the first doctor in his entire year here to show any real interest in staying. And he needed her skills. But could he count on her coming through, the way he'd counted on Nancy before she'd let him down?

He didn't know, couldn't tell. Juliette was obviously of upper means and, yes, that did have a huge bearing on the way he was feeling so uneasy about her motives or dedication. But there was also something about her that caused him to believe that her upper means hadn't knocked something basic out of her. She was a hard worker and, so far, she hadn't complained about the menial tasks. Time would tell what she was really made of, he supposed. For now, he was simply trying to keep an open mind. Because for some reason other than his need of her medical skills, a reason he couldn't quite put his finger on, he wanted her to stay. Maybe for a change of scenery? Or to break the monotony? He honestly didn't know.

"You've only got just the one exam room in

the clinic?" Juliette asked him, once all the beds were made.

"The clinic was originally my living quarters. One room for everything. But I built a divider so there would be a waiting room on one side and an exam room on the other. That's all there was room for."

"Then where do you sleep?" she asked him.

"In a hut next door. Another one-room setup. Not as nice as the hospital, though."

Juliette cringed. "I hate to ask, but where will I stay when I'm here?"

Ah, yes. The first test. No sheets, no bed—no room of her own. This is where it began, he supposed. Or ended. "Well, I've got two choices. You could stay here in the hospital, use an empty bed and hope we don't get so busy you'll have to give it up. We'll partition it off for you to give you some privacy. And the perk there is that the hospital has running water, a shower, a bathroom. Or, if you don't like that idea, you can shack with me. And the drawbacks there are—I don't have running water, don't have a bathroom or a shower. I have to come into the hospital for all that. Oh, and rumor has it that I might snore." He cringed, waiting for what he believed would be the inevitable.

"So if I choose your hut, I'd be what? Sleeping in bed with you?"

"No, I'm a little more gentlemanly than that. I'd give you the bed, and I'd take the floor." Said with some forced humor, since humor was all he had to offer at the moment.

"But in the same room?"

"Kind of like the student years, when you'd crash in the on-call room, no matter who was sleeping next to you. You did sleep in an on-call, didn't you?" Somehow, he could picture Juliette as the type who would lock the on-call door behind her and keep the room all to herself.

"I did," she said hesitantly. "When I had to."

"So let me guess. You didn't like it."

"It was necessary, when I was pulling twenty-four-hour shifts. But did I like it? Not particularly."

"How did I know that?" he asked, still waiting for the curtain to fall on this little act he was putting on. Who was he kidding here? Girls accustomed to silk sheets liked silk. And he sure as hell didn't have anything silk.

"You *didn't* know that," she said, expelling an exasperated sigh. "You're just into making snap judgments about me. All of them negative. Do you *ever* see anything positive in *any* situation, Damien?"

Maybe she was right. Maybe he was so used to looking for the negative that he wouldn't recognize a ray of something positive if it walked right up and slapped him in the face. Damn, he didn't mean to be like that. But something about Juliette poked at him. It was almost like he was trying to push her away. From what? He had no clue. "Look, I'll try to be more positive, OK?"

"Don't put yourself out on my account. I'm a big girl. I can take it." She squared herself up to her full five-foot-six frame and stared him down. "And I think I'll just stay in the hospital, all things considered." Narrowing her eyes, she went on, "I *hate* snoring. And, just for the record, Damien, you're not going to scare me off. I came here so I could stay better in touch with patient care, and I don't intend to back out of it, no matter how hard you're trying to push me away."

"I'm not trying to push you away," he defended.

"Sure you are. Don't know why, don't particularly care. Just let me do my job here, and we'll get along. OK?"

Well, she certainly was driven. He liked that. Liked it a lot. "Look, if you want privacy, you can have my hut on the weekends you're here, and I'll stay in the hospital."

"The weekends I'm here will be every weekend."

"You're sure of that? Because it's a long, tough drive to get here, and I don't have anything to make your life, or your work, easier when you're here."

"I'm adaptable, Damien. I'll make do."

He wanted to trust that she would. "Look, we can finish talking about your housing options later on, over dinner. But, right now, Señor Mendez is waiting in the clinic. Remember, gout? Oh, and I'm going to go make a house call. I have a patient who's a week over her due date, and she's getting pretty anxious to have her baby."

"Borrow my car. Take her for a ride on that bumpy road into town. That should induce something."

So she had a sense of humor. Even though she made her offer with a straight face, Damien laughed. "Might work better if I borrow a cart and a donkey from one of the locals."

"They actually have donkey carts here?" she asked in full amazement.

"It's called traveling in style. A modern convenience if the cart is fairly new and the donkey is reasonably young." He stopped himself short of ridiculing the kind of car she probably had back home. A sleek sports model, most likely. Shiny and silver. Convertible. Her hair let down from its ponytail and blowing in the breeze. Nope, he had to stop this. It was going too far, almost daydreaming about her the way he was. "Anyway, I'll probably be back before you're done with Señor Mendez's toe."

"Will Alegria be able to unlock the medicine cabinet for me?"

Before he answered, he fished through the pocket of his khaki cargo shorts until he found a key. "Here, take mine. Just make sure you give it back before you leave here—when? Sunday night? Monday morning?"

"Haven't decided yet. I guess it will depend on the workload."

He dropped the key into her outstretched hand.

"Well, next time I get to Cima de la Montaña I'll have a key made for you." Provided she lasted that long. In a lot of ways, he hoped she did because, in spite of himself, and especially in spite of all his doubts, he liked her.

CHAPTER THREE

"HOW WAS YOUR gout patient?" Damien asked Juliette on his way back into the hospital. She was coming out of the clinic, looking somewhat perplexed. "It *was* gout, wasn't it?"

"It was gout," Juliette confirmed. "I was concerned about his age, though. He seems too young to be afflicted with it."

"I thought so, too, but the people here live hard lives. They age faster than normal."

"And he's had a complete physical?"

"Before he presented with gout symptoms?" Damien shook his head. "Getting people around here to submit to physicals when they don't have any particular symptoms isn't easy, but about six months ago Señor Mendez did come in. Nothing out of the ordinary turned up."

"Well, I gave him aspirin like you told me to. But there was something else going on. I think Señor Mendez was high on some kind of drug. At least, that's the way he seemed. Slurred speech, slow movements. Do you know if he indulges?"

Damien laughed. "A lot of the locals indulge. I'm surprised Señor Mendez would, though. He's pretty straight. Doesn't drink that I know of. Doesn't do drugs—at least, I didn't think he did. And, even if he did, it surprises me that he would go out in public that way because he's a very polite, private, gentle man who spends every last penny he has to support his family. But I guess you never know what goes on behind closed doors, do you?"

"Is it really that common around here?"

"Ganja—marijuana—is cheap, and easily available."

"So what do you do if they come in here stoned?"

"Treat them for what they came in for, and ignore the rest. I'm just the doctor here. I don't get involved in anything else."

"Then you won't report him?"

"If he's not bothering me, there's no reason to. My personal policy is, if someone needs help they get help, in spite of all the external factors that might otherwise cause problems. In other words, if he's stoned, you treat him, anyway. The rest of it's none of my business."

"That's decent of you."

"I aim to be decent to my patients. They've got enough hardships to face in their daily lives without me adding to them."

"But do you condone it?"

"Nope. I'm a law-abiding citizen wherever I go, and the Costa Rican law makes ganja illegal, so I respect that."

"Then you, personally, don't indulge?"

"Never have, never will. Don't smoke, either. Drink only in moderation. Work out regularly. Eat a balanced diet. You know, all good things for my body." A body that seemed to be aging too quickly since he'd come to Costa Rica. Of course, that was about the hard work here. So were the new creases in his face and the pair of glasses he was now forced to wear any time he wanted to read. Most people wouldn't consider him old, as he overtook his thirty-sixth birthday in a few weeks. But some days he just felt old—older than dirt. "Keeps me in good working condition."

"Well, I just wanted to let you know the condition of your patient."

"And I appreciate that. But I'm not really concerned about it. At least, not right now."

"When does that point change for you, Damien?"

"When I see someone's drug use as a potential danger to themselves or others. That's when I'll step in. But again, only as a doctor."

"We always had to note it in our chart at the hospital," she said. "And if it was too bad, we were supposed to alert Security."

"Did you ever?"

"Once. Then I had regrets, because he really wasn't that bad. But I was new, still blindly loyal to hospital policy, probably more so than to the patient. Of course, that changed pretty quickly, the more involved I became with my patients."

"So you were a true, big hospital loyalist?"

"Still am. But I'm more practical about it now. But you've got to understand that I was raised by a true hospital loyalist—the chief of staff, and those were the kinds of concerns he always brought home with him. What was best for the hospital was always his main concern, right after the kind of patient care we were giving."

"So your daddy's a big shot in a big hospital?"

Given her rich girl background, that didn't surprise him.

"That's one way of putting it, I suppose. But to me he was always just my dad. A man who went to work, worked long, hard hours and came home to tuck me in every night. It never occurred to me that he was so important in terms of an entire medical community until I was probably ten or eleven and he took me to work with him to see what he did during the day."

"Did it impress you?"

"Not so much then. I think I was more impressed by all the desserts in the cafeteria than I was by my father's position in the hospital. Of course, the older I got the more I realized just what a *big deal* he was."

"But you have no aspirations for something like that for yourself?"

"I had my shot at it. Dad offered me a promotion into administration a couple of months ago."

"So let me guess. You chose Costa Rica instead. Was it to run away from Daddy?" Probably her first real act of rebellion in a very laid-out life.

"You say that like it was a derogatory thing to do."

"Was it?" he asked her.

Juliette shook her head. "I like to think of Costa Rica as something necessary in my career development. In my personal development, as well. Also, I didn't feel as though I'd earned the job. I think promoting me was simply my dad's way of ensuring that I'd stay around for a while. Or forever, if he had his way about it. I mean, my dad always wins. No matter what it is, he finds a way to win, and I was tired of always having my ideas and hopes and desires tossed into that lottery."

Actually, that was admirable. "So you *did* want to get away from Daddy." He liked the kind of spirit it must have taken for her to make that much of a change in her life—a life that was, apparently, very sheltered. Something Nancy would have never done for anyone, for any reason.

"I wanted to get away from all the usual trappings and…"

"Make it on your own merits rather than resting on the laurels your dad created for you?"

"Do you challenge all the women you come into contact with, or is it just *me* who challenges *you*?"

He thought about that for a moment, wondering

if his leftover resentment of Nancy did, adversely, affect his relationships with women. Certainly, he hadn't dated since Nancy. Not once. Not even tempted. No one-night stands. No quick meet-ups at the coffee shop. No phone calls, texting or any other sort of personal communications. In fact, if anything, he assiduously avoided *everything* that came close to putting him into a relationship of any sort with any woman—young, old or somewhere in between.

"Actually, you haven't challenged me yet. But I'm sure you're waiting for the right opportunity."

Juliette laughed. "You won't see it coming," she warned him. "And you'll be caught so far off guard, you won't know what hit you."

Now, that was something he could foresee happening. Juliette had a very disarming way about her, and he had every inclination to believe that she was good at the sneak attack. Of course, he was the one who'd placed himself directly in her line of fire, and he still didn't understand why he'd done that. But he was there, nonetheless, actually looking forward to her first barrage of arrows. "Sounds like the lady has a plan."

"My only plan is to take the next patient, who's

coming through the door right now." She gave him a devious smile. "Unless you're really into doing some stitches today." A snap diagnosis made with the assumption that underneath the bloody towel the mother was holding over her son's hand lay something that needed stitching. "You *do* have a suture kit, don't you?"

He turned around, also looked at the people coming through the hospital door. Diego Cruz and his mother, Elena. This wasn't the first time Diego had needed stitches, and it wouldn't be the last as Diego was an active little boy who was pretty much left to run wild through Bombacopsis while his mother cooked and cleaned and sewed for other villagers.

Elena was one of Damien's regular hospital volunteers as well, which took even more time away from Diego. "If you mean needles and thread, yep, I've got them." He waved at Diego, who gave him a limp wave in return.

"Regulars?"

Damien chuckled as he bent to greet the little boy. "One of our best. So, Diego. What happened here?"

"I fell," the child confessed.

"From the top of the gate at the church," Elena volunteered.

"Were you trying to break in again?" Damien asked him, fighting to keep a straight face.

"Only for a drink of water."

"You couldn't go home for that?"

"It was too far." Diego looked up at Juliette and turned on a rather charming smile. "And the water at the church is holy, which is good for me. It makes me grow stronger."

"Well, you weren't strong enough to keep yourself from falling off the gate, were you?" Damien took the towel off the boy's hand and had a look. It wasn't a bad cut, not too deep, but deep enough that it would take about four or five stitches. The same number of stitches he'd had in his other hand a month ago, when he'd tried to remove the log bridge that crossed the village creek, and had gotten hung up on it.

"That's because I didn't have my drink yet."

Diego reminded Damien a lot of himself when he'd been that age. He and his twin, Daniel, were always getting into some kind of trouble. Nothing serious, but usually with some consequence like a broken arm, a sprained ankle, multiple areas of stitches. “You seem to have all the answers, Diego,” he said, finally giving way to a laugh.

“I try, el doctor Damien,” Diego responded earnestly.

“Well, here’s the deal. I’m going to go get you that drink of water, from the hospital faucet, *not* from the church. And, while you’re waiting for me to bring it back to you, el doctor Juliette is going to take care of your hand. Which means you’re going to get stitches like you had last month. Remember?”

Diego nodded his head. “They hurt,” he said, looking up at his mother as if she was going to stop the procedure. “Do I have to?” he asked her.

“You have to do whatever el doctor Damien says,” his mother told him. “He’s the boss.”

For a moment Diego looked defeated. Then he perked right back up. “But el doctor Damien won’t hurt me much. That’s what he promised me last time.”

“Hey, Diego. This one could have hurt a lot more if you’d cut something other than your hand,” Damien said. He raised up and looked at Juliette. “Suture material’s in the third drawer in the clinic cabinet. Oh, and I do have xylocaine to deaden the pain. I keep a fair stock of it on hand, thanks to Diego, here. He's our main consumer."

"Sure you don't want to do this, since you and Diego seemed to have built a rapport?" she asked. "He might trust you more."

"No, I'll let you do it. Even at the tender age of ten, our man here has an eye for the pretty ladies, and I'm sure he'd much rather have you taking care of him. Isn't that right, Diego?"

Once again, Diego turned his smile on for Juliette. "Right," he said, scooting past his mother and stepping closer to Juliette. "El doctor Juliette is very pretty."

Damien shrugged. "Like I said…"

"OK, Romeo," Juliette said to Diego, as she took his unwounded hand and led him into the exam room. "Let's see what we can do about fixing this up."

"My name is Diego, *not* Romeo!" he said defiantly.

"Where she comes from, they mean the same thing," Damien said from the doorway.

Juliette flashed Damien a knowing look. "Where I come from, grown women never have to worry about advances from ten-year-old boys."

"Almost eleven," Diego corrected. He closed his eyes while Juliette swabbed his hand clean in order to take a closer look at his cut.

"Does it hurt much?" Juliette asked, accepting a cotton gauze pad Damien had fished out of a drawer for her.

"No," Diego said. But the slight tentativeness in his voice said otherwise.

"Diego is one tough little kid," Damien said, on his way to the closet to fetch the xylocaine. "And the shot that el doctor Juliette is about to give him won't hurt at all, will it, Diego?"

This time his tentativeness was full-blown. "No," he said, pulling back his hand slightly.

"You going to break into the church again, Diego? Because this is the second time in a month and it's not going to be too long before Padre Benicio comes after you."

Diego's eyes opened wide. "Will he hurt me?" he asked.

"No, he won't hurt you. But he'll make you do chores, like washing the windows, or cleaning up the church garden." Damien recalled how he and Daniel had been the recipient of such chores from time to time. "And if you come in here hurt again because you've done something bad, I'm going to make you pay for your medical treatment with some chores here. Like painting the fence outside, or scrubbing the floors."

"I think he means it, Diego," Juliette said as she turned to hide the smile crossing her face. "By the way, does he need a tetanus shot? And I'm assuming you *do* offer that?"

"I *do* offer that, as a matter of fact. But Diego is up-to-date. I got him a couple of months ago when he got into a fight with a fence of chicken wire." Damien liked Diego. A lot. He was a smart kid. Resourceful. Bright in school. Knew how to get along in his own little world. But he didn't have a father, which meant his mother had to work doubly hard to support her small family. That, more than anything else, contributed to the mischief that always seemed to find Diego. The kid simply had too much time on his hands.

"Hey, Diego," Damien said, suddenly finding a little bit of inspiration, "I have an idea. Are you interested?"

"Maybe," Diego said, not even noticing that Juliette was preparing the syringe to give him the xylocaine shot.

"OK, well…" Damien blinked, sympathizing with the kid while Juliette stuck the needle into his hand. The hand was sensitive and that shot had to hurt, but Diego merely flinched and bit down on his lower lip. "Want a job?"

"A job, el doctor Damien?"

"Yes, a job. Here, in the hospital."

"For real money?"

Out of his own pocket, if he had to, Damien decided. This kid needed better direction. That was something he could do, without too much effort. "Real money."

Juliette threaded the suture needle and turned Diego's hand at a more convenient angle before she proceeded to start stitching. "You could make beds," she suggested, smiling over at Damien.

"No, I have something better than that in mind," Damien responded, smiling back.

"Could I be el doctor Diego?" Diego asked.

"Not until you're older, and have had more schooling. But you could be the person in charge of el doctor Damien's files."

Juliette raised amused eyebrows. "Now, that seems like a fitting job. And a very important one."

Damien nodded his agreement. "I can teach

Diego how to alphabetize, then he can keep things filed away in proper order. I mean, we do it the old-fashioned way here. Paper notes put into folders, sorted and put away in the file cabinet. Everything completely organized."

"I can organize," Diego said.

"Do you even know what organized means?" Juliette asked him.

"No, but el doctor Damien will teach me."

She looked at Damien. "He has a lot of confidence in you."

Truth was, Damien had a lot of confidence in Diego. He wanted to be a good kid, and he tried hard to do it, but too many times his circumstances simply got in his way. Damien's own father had been the influence that had kept him from becoming too out of control, and Damien hoped he could be that same influence for Diego.

"Elena," he directed at Diego's mother. "Is it all right that Diego works for me?"

"That would be very good," she said, excitement registering on her face. "He responds very well to you and maybe this will help keep him out of trouble."

"Good, then I'll make out a schedule in a little

while, and maybe Diego could start working tomorrow. OK with you, Diego?" he asked, shifting his attention back to the boy.

"For real money!" Diego exclaimed, as Juliette sank her first stitch.

Damien gave him a thumbs-up.

"Maybe I'll buy a car!" Diego exclaimed, grinning from ear to ear.

"You have real money to give him?" Juliette asked Damien, after Diego had gone skipping out of the hospital, bragging to one of the volunteers on the way that he was going to have a *real* job here, at the hospital.

"I have a little bit of money put away. And it won't take much to keep Diego happy. Five hundred *colónes* a week come to little less than a dollar, and that's not going to break my bank."

Juliette was impressed. More than impressed; she was touched by the way he'd handled Diego. He was a natural with children. And his love of children shone through so brilliantly it almost surprised her, as she hadn't expected to see that from him. "Do you have kids of your own?" she asked him.

"Never married, never had children."

"Is that your avowed way of life, or just something that has occurred because of your restless lifestyle? Because, if you ever truly settled down, I think you'd make a wonderful dad."

"Not a wonderful husband, too?" he asked, grinning at her.

He did have his good qualities. Juliette was beginning to see that. But did he have enough to make him good husband material? For her, the answer was no. For someone else—it all depended on what they wanted, or didn't want, in a husband. "Since you've never been married, there's no way to tell. And, personally, I'd never get that involved with you to find out."

"Never?" he asked.

"Outside of a professional relationship, *never.*"

"That's harsh."

"But honest." She knew he was teasing her now, and that was a side of him she quite liked. Apart from his ability with children, maybe there were some other redeemable qualities in him after all.

"Said by a lady who, if I'm not mistaken, has never been married herself."

"Never married. No regrets about it, either."

"For now," he countered.

"For now, maybe for the rest of my life." She didn't think about it much, to be honest. What was the point? If it happened, it happened. If didn't, it didn't. Dwelling on the *what ifs* didn't get her anywhere.

"Because you want more than any man could possibly give you?"

"Because I want what I want, and I haven't found it yet." It was a simple statement, but oh, so true. She hadn't come close to finding what she wanted. Funny thing was, she couldn't exactly define what it was. Couldn't put it into a mental checklist, couldn't even put it down on paper it was so vague to her. Yet she truly believed that if the man who fit her undefined list came into her life, everything would become crystal clear to her. She'd know him. She'd see the qualities that, until that very moment, had been nothing but a nebulous notion.

The day passed fairly quickly, and Damien was glad to see that it was finally turning into night. People had wandered in and out all day long, none of them with serious complaints, but now he expected they would stay home, coming to the hospital only if it was an emergency. Kicking back in a chair in the hospital waiting room, he put his feet up on a small side table, clasped his hands behind his neck and stretched back, sighing. "We don't usually see too much action at night. The people here like to eat a good dinner and go to bed early."

"The *arroz con pollo* certainly qualifies as a good dinner," Juliette commented, taking a seat across from Damien. "I love chicken and rice. Probably could eat it every few days."

"Which is how often you're going to get it here. The hospital is pretty limited in its culinary offerings, and we rely mostly on what the locals donate to us. They all raise chickens, rice is cheap, so—*arroz con pollo* happens a lot."

"Maybe I can get Rosalita's recipe for it. My roommate and I trade off on the cooking chores, and most of the time I just fix sandwiches and salads. She might enjoy something different from me, for a change."

"Do you like to cook?"

Juliette shook her head. "I've always had someone to do the cooking for me. Or I ate out. But now I work such crazy hours, it's easier to stay in to eat, because when I finally do get home I'm not inclined to go back out just for food."

"So you had a maid to change your bed, *and* a cook to fix your meals. Any other servants?"

"They weren't servants, Damien. Nobody calls them that! They were just employees. People who worked for us."

"Then I stand corrected. Did you have other people who worked for you?"

"Just a gardener, and he was only part-time."

"And someone to tend your pool?"

"We had a pool," she admitted. "And someone did tend to it."

"So we're up to four people who worked for you. Anybody else? Maybe a tailor for your dad, or a personal assistant to keep your calendar organized."

"OK, so we hired people to work for us. What of it?"

"Nothing, really. I'm just trying to determine the extent of your wealth." It was late, he was tired, yet here he was, baiting her again. Something about Juliette brought that out in him; he didn't want to be intentionally cruel to her, but his need to raise her hackles just seemed to ooze out of him, no matter how hard he tried to stop.

"And here I thought you were trying to be civil with me." Juliette pushed herself up out of the chair. "Look, I'm not in the mood to go another round with you tonight. So, I'm just going out to the ward, find myself an empty bed and go to sleep. If you need me— You know what? I don't want you coming to get me. Send one of the volunteers to do it."

"It was an honest question, Juliette. I was simply trying to find out more about you." *Yeah, right.* More like he was just trying to find out how far he could push her before she pushed back. In a sense, it was vital to her work here and how much he could throw at her before she resisted him. Of course, it was also about taunting her, which was something he was going to have to quit doing. If he wanted her to come back, and he did, he needed to be nicer to her. Needed to quit testing her. Most of all, he needed to stop comparing her to Nancy because she definitely *wasn't* anything like Nancy.

"Well, I'm not in the mood for your honesty."

Damien did like the way she stood up for herself. "But honesty is one of my best virtues. I don't lie. Not about anything. And if I want to know something, I ask."

"Well, you can ask me anything you want, professionally. But my personal life is out of it because you've prejudged who I am and what I am, and I can't see you being the type who changes his mind once it's made up."

She was right about that. "OK, so let me be honest here. I have a bias against wealthy people. More specifically, spoiled rich girls." So now she knew. In a way that was good, as it gave them a base to work from. And he really did want a better footing with Juliette, no matter how much he acted toward the contrary.

"You think I'm spoiled?"

"Are you?" he asked.

Juliette huffed out an impatient breath. "I've had advantages most other people don't have, and I'll admit that. And I'll also admit that I've enjoyed the privilege that comes from my father's wealth. So to you that may scream spoiled, but to me it says normal. Everything that I've achieved or had or done is normal to me. If you think that's being spoiled, then think it. It's not worth the effort of trying to change your mind, because I simply don't care what you think of me personally. Go ahead and label me all you want, if that's what makes you feel good. But don't waste my time pointing it out to me, because I've got better things to worry about. Like the job I intend to do here, no matter how bad you treat me."

She was red and fiery when she was angry. And sexy as hell! He liked that. Liked it a lot. "Look, I have these preconceived ideas, right or wrong, and for those, I do apologize. I'm trying to get that under control. But I also have an irascible personality that needs attention, which I haven't had time to give it."

"Irascible?"

"You know. Hot-tempered. Irritable."

"Yes, I've noticed. And you freely admit that?"

"I do because, like I said, I'm honest."

"Do you like being irascible?"

"Not so much." Especially now. But it overtook him and sometimes he couldn't control it. Like with Juliette. It was part of his restlessness, he supposed.

"Then stop it. You're a smart man. You're capable of getting a grip on yourself, if you want to.

So quit acting like you're so mean because, deep down, I don't think you really are. It's only a defense mechanism, Damien. Against what, I don't know. Don't want to know. But if you keep putting people off, the way you do, you're going to wind up in a Costa Rican jungle with no friends, and no place to go. That could turn out to be very sad for you."

She was softening now, her flare of anger dying down. This smoother side of her was so attractive, all he wanted to do was stay in that place, at that time, and stare at her. But there was a part of Juliette that scared him—the part that was so easily digging beneath his surface to discover who he really was. Most of the time, he kept that face hidden. Didn't want people getting close because, in his experience, people who could find the vulnerable place had the power to hurt. Nancy had hurt him. In spite of all the things he'd seen in her, and all the qualms he'd had about marrying someone coming from an indulged, wealthy background, he'd still planned a life with her. In fact, he'd tried hard to make the changes she'd needed to see in him, changes he didn't necessarily want to make but had made, nonetheless, because that was what she'd wanted.

In essence, he'd been true to Nancy but he hadn't been true to himself. No way was he going to do that again, so it was easier to push people away before they expected something of him.

"There could be worse things than ending up here without friends and no place to go," he said, even though a big chunk of him didn't believe that.

"Look, Damien. You're fighting some kind of battle here, and apparently you've decided to drag me into it. But I never fight. Not with you, not with anybody. All I want is for you to lay off the snide remarks and let me do my work. You don't have to like me, I don't have to like you. And it seems we're starting out that way, which doesn't make a working relationship easy, but since I'm only going to be here a couple days a week, our feelings about each other shouldn't get in the way. If you want to run me off, don't do it because I rub you the wrong way. Or because I'm wealthy. Do it because my work isn't good enough. Do it because I have a lousy bedside manner. Do it because I'm not as good of a doctor as you need. But don't do it because of personal issues. OK?

Oh, and don't cop out to an excuse like your self-admitted irascible nature because, frankly, I don't care what you are by nature. All I want is a good supervisor. Someone who will help me when I need it, and leave me alone when I don't. And someone who doesn't ridicule me because I don't know how to make a bed."

Man, oh, man, *had* he been wrong when he'd compared Juliette to Nancy. Nancy would have never stood up to him like that. She was quiet, always ran to Daddy and Daddy did the talking. And she would have never been as passionate about anything the way Juliette was passionate about working here.

"You know. We're both tired. We've had a long day and we've got another long day ahead of us tomorrow. This is new to you, and you're new to me, both of which are going to take some getting used to. So maybe we should just stop this right here. You can go get some sleep. I'll hang around for another hour or so, do some final bed checks, turn the rest of the night over to George Perkins and go back to my hut and grab a couple hours of sleep. Then we'll regroup in the morning and see what we've got."

"Who's George Perkins?" she asked.

"My other doctor here. Plastic surgeon, good man. A little burned-out on medicine, but working his way back in."

"Burned-out?"

"He substituted work for life." The way *he* did. "Lost his wife over it, but one of the women here—let's just say that the love of a good woman has worked miracles for him. He's finding a new purpose."

"Well, here's to the good women," she said.

"They are out there, I suppose."

"You *suppose*?"

"Did I offend you again?"

"Actually, you didn't. And you didn't surprise me, either."

"Good. Then I don't have anything else to apologize for."

"Maybe, before you do, I should just go find myself a bed and stay away from you for a while."

If there was any way he could make this situation any more tense between them he sure couldn't come up with what it might be. It was as if to open his mouth was to say something he didn't intend to say. Hell of it was, he couldn't seem to stop himself. But tomorrow—ah, yes, the great unknown tomorrow. He wanted to think that come tomorrow he'd do better. Truth was, though, he didn't know if he could.

"Look, I've got a couple of room dividers stashed in the supply closet. Let me go get them and section you off from the rest of the ward. It's not much in the way of privacy, but it's the best I've got."

Juliette nodded her agreement and managed a polite smile. "Tomorrow will be better," she told him.

He hoped that would be true. "Let's keep our fingers crossed."

"So what time do you want me on in the morning?"

Damien checked his watch. It was almost midnight now, and breakfast would be served at seven thirty. "I'll have George wake you up at six. That should give you enough time to shower and get ready."

"Get ready for what?"

"Didn't I tell you? Rosalita doesn't come in until it's time to cook the noon meal. We all pitch in so I'm putting you in charge of the kitchen for breakfast."

"You've got to be kidding!"

Damien smiled at her. "It beats bedsheets, doesn't it?"

CHAPTER FOUR

JULIETTE TOSSED AND turned for almost an hour before she finally dozed off. The bed was lumpy, the sheets scratchy and the patient down the row from her snored like a buzz saw. None of that mattered much, as her mind was focused on Damien. Images of him popped up behind her eyelids when she closed her eyes, thoughts of him sent her brain into overload, instantly awakening every synapse in her body. But why?

Well, she wasn't sure. Maybe because he was an enigma of a man. It was as if he ran hot and cold, minute to minute. Nice then cutting, all in a flash. To say the least, it was peculiar behavior. But she wasn't going to criticize him for it, even though in the span of only one day she'd become the target of his off-and-on belligerence, as if something was boiling just underneath his surface. She didn't have to look too hard to see it.

"You're Juliette, aren't you?" A man with a very

thick Boston accent poked his head in around her partition. "Damien told me to wake you up if I needed help."

"What time is it?" she asked groggily.

"A little after two. And I hate to disturb you like this, but one of us has got to go down the road and deliver a baby while the other one stays here and looks after the hospital."

"Are you George Perkins?" she asked as she tried to shake her single hour of sleep off her stiff body.

"Yes," he said. "George Perkins, plastic surgeon in the States, GP in the jungle, at your service. Pleased to make your acquaintance, Juliette. Sorry this comes at such a bad time but, in my experience, most of the babies I've delivered here have preferred to make their grand entrance in the middle of the night."

Juliette switched on her bedside light to have a good look at him. He was a distinguished man with silver hair and a full gray beard. He sported a crisp linen shirt and a neatly pressed pair of khaki trousers, looking very much as if he could have stepped right off the pages of a fashion magazine. All in all, he was a good-looking gent.

And he looked…happy. Something she'd never seen in her father, and had never even seen in herself when she looked in the mirror. "Damien didn't mention that I was to be on call tonight. Is it posted somewhere that I should have noticed?"

"Damien doesn't mention a lot of things. You'll get used to that if you stay with us for very long. Also, we don't post things around here because most of the volunteers barely speak English and they sure as heck can't read it. So, everything's passed down directly, from person to person. As for taking calls at night, in my current situation which, in case Damien didn't tell you, is I'm living with a very lovely village woman and I prefer working nights while Carmelita and her children are sleeping, so no one really has to take calls then, unless I'm taking a night off. I'm just hoping that you'll stand in as my backup right now because I don't want to go wake Damien up to help me. He was on thirty-six hours straight before tonight, and he needs his rest."

Juliette blew out a deep breath and sat up. "So what do you want me to do? Deliver a baby, or watch the hospital?"

"Do you like babies?" he asked her. "Because if

you do, I'd rather stay here and attend to a couple of my regulars who like to come see me in the middle of the night."

"Sure, no problem." Juliette swung her legs over the side of the bed and stood up. Normally, at home, she'd be wearing pajamas. But here, in the jungle, she'd brought a pair of scrubs along as she didn't know what she'd be doing and scrubs were good everyday work clothes, as well as stand-in pajamas. "Where can I find the mother-to-be?"

"Down this road until you get to the church. Turn left at that intersection, go another block, then turn right. She'll be in the third house on the left. The best landmark I can give you is a rusted-out old pickup truck in her front yard, and the house should be well lit, as half the village usually turns out for a birth." He held out a flashlight. "No streetlights," he said sheepishly.

House calls by flashlight. Couldn't say she'd ever done anything like that before, but there was a first time for everything. So she took the light from him and switched it on to make sure the batteries were good. They were. "Any complications? Anything I should know about before I go?"

"Her name is Maria Salas, and this is her third child so it should be a fairly easy birth. She hasn't been in labor long, according to her husband, but he thinks the baby is coming quickly. Apparently, she has a history of fast births."

"Then I should get going," Juliette said, bending down to pull on her sneakers. "Do you have a medical kit with maternity supplies I can take along with me?"

"I put it by the front door before I came to get you. It should have everything you need for a straightforward birth. But if you run into any complications, have one of Maria's family members run and fetch Damien."

"Will do." Juliette pushed herself off the bed and headed immediately toward the door. She was finally awake, still feeling a little sluggish, though, as one hour hadn't been enough to shake off her tiredness. "Should we try to get her into the hospital for this? Because I'm not sure a home delivery is the safest thing to do." Also, as director of a clinic, she'd never made a house call in her life, flashlight or not, and, while she was looking forward to the experience, it also made her a little nervous going so far outside of what she'd ever done. But that was what they did here, and she was part of it now. So it was what she did, too.

"Sure. Bring her in, if she can make it. But I doubt that's going to work out for you because most of the women here prefer home births. You know, have the baby then getting back onto whatever they were doing before it came."

That was a stamina Juliette admired. As for her, though, if she ever had a baby, she wanted it in a modern hospital with all the latest equipment. Wanted an anesthesiologist on hand to give her an epidural for the pain. Wanted fetal monitors, and heart monitors, and blood pressure monitors. Soft lights and soft music in the delivery room.

"Well, whatever happens, if she's as fast about it as you've been led to believe, maybe I'll be able to get back here in time to grab another couple hours of sleep."

"Or you can sleep in the morning, when Damien comes on."

Right. And listen to Damien taunt her about that for the next several weeks. *What did you do? Come to the jungle just to sleep?*

Juliette grabbed the rucksack by the door and

fairly ran out and on down the street, flashing her light along the path, making the proper turns where she needed and continuing on until she came to the rusty old truck standing in Maria's front yard. It was surrounded by several people, who were all talking quite loudly, as if they were having a party. Indeed, half the village seemed to be there, as George had said.

"The baby's coming out now," one of the men told her. "My new grandchild."

"And it's going to be a big baby. Maria always has big babies," an older woman added.

Juliette's first thought was gestational diabetes. It was a condition that put the mother and child at some degree of risk, and usually resulted in larger than the average baby. But hadn't Damien been seeing Maria? Surely, he would have noticed such a condition and prepared for it. Also, George would have mentioned it to her. So Juliette put that notion out of her head, preferring to think that Maria had received excellent prenatal care from Damien. In spite of his attitude, everything she'd seen and read about him told her he was a good doctor. "Thank you," she said, scooting past all the gathered people and hurrying through Maria's open front door.

The lights were bright inside, revealing a clean but cluttered little house. Judging from the knick-knacks, toys, books, small appliances and clothing strewn everywhere, the Salas family never came across an object of any sort that they couldn't collect. "Where is she?" she asked one of the five people huddled among the clutter.

"Back bedroom, left side of the hall. Go through the kitchen." The man pointed to a narrow pathway winding its way through a corridor of old chairs, tables and lamps.

Juliette squeezed through the maze and stopped just short of entering the kitchen. "What are *you* doing here?" she asked.

Damien, who was sitting in an old chrome chair at the kitchen table, smiled up at her. "Same thing you are, I guess."

"They came and got you, too?"

He shrugged. "I'm her doctor. Who else would they call?"

"Me."

"Not sure why they'd do that, seeing as how you've never even met Maria."

"George Perkins woke me up. Told me to get down here."

"George overreacts sometimes."

"Like sending me here in the middle of the night when I could be back at the hospital, sleeping?"

"I could be saying the same thing. But I started to realize, probably in my first couple of days here, that people's needs were always going to supersede my sleep. Comes with the territory."

"Well, that's too bad for you, I suppose."

"I'm used to it." He stretched back in his chair. "Anyway, Maria's fully dilated, fully effaced. Pushing it out as we speak."

"Then shouldn't you be in there, delivering the baby instead of sitting here, casually talking about it?" Frankly, she was shocked that he wasn't more involved at this stage.

"I'd like to be, but Maria's mother and grandmother are in there, along with her two sisters, a couple of cousins and an aunt. There's really no room for anyone else."

"You mean no room for a doctor?"

"She's already got plenty of help standing by. She doesn't need a doctor."

He was being so blithely unconcerned about

this, it surprised her. "But haven't you been seeing her all along?"

"I was here earlier today, as a matter of fact. Kind of thought the baby would be coming in the next day or so."

"And yet you're sitting here, doing nothing."

"Actually, I'm sitting here, waiting to take over if she starts having problems. That's the only reason they called us in—as backups. Luckily, though, she's progressing through a normal delivery quite nicely. Oh, and I do poke my head in the door every few minutes to check on how things are going."

"So who's going to actually deliver the baby?"

"Her grandmother. She's delivered more babies than I have. I know she delivered Maria's first two. Oh, and just last week she delivered her neighbor's baby." He shrugged. "Lady's got a lot of experience, and she resents anybody barging in who doesn't belong there. In Irene's opinion, *we* do not belong there."

"Then she's a midwife," Juliette stated, relieved that someone with experience and knowledge was taking over.

"Of sorts. I mean she's not trained or anything

like that. She's just always available to do something she's been doing for sixty years."

Sixty years? That alarmed Juliette. "How old is she?"

"Not sure, since she doesn't go to doctors or hospitals, and we don't have her records. But I'm guessing she's somewhere around eighty, give or take a few years."

"Eighty and still delivering babies? Why do you allow that, Damien? You're the doctor in this village. Shouldn't you have some say in the medical concerns of the people who live here?"

"Normally, I do. But when it comes to childbirth, the women here gang up on me and keep me at a distance. It's their tradition to rally around their mothers in labor and see to the delivery. They've been doing it for more years than the two of us combined have been here on this earth. So who am I to intrude?"

Juliette pushed her hair back from her face. Tonight, it wasn't banded up in a ponytail. "Do you think they'd mind if I looked in?"

"As another woman, or as a doctor?"

"Why can't I be both?"

Damien laughed. “You really can’t be that naive, can you?”

“What do you mean by that?”

“These people practiced their folk medicine long before anything remotely modern came in and took over, and so many of the older ones still hold on to their old ways. They’ll tolerate us when they need us, but otherwise they’ll resist the hell out of what we try to offer them because they consider that an insult. People trust what they know, and resist anything new to them. The fine art of healing is included in that.”

From somewhere behind the wall to her right, the quiet voices of people chattering were beginning to grow louder, and Juliette wondered if that was a sign of imminent birth. The ladies in the room with Maria were getting excited. She could almost picture them huddling around the bed, talking, as Maria was assuming the position to deliver. All so casual. “Well, resistance or not, I’m going to go take a peek.”

“Or you could sit down with me here, have a nice *refresco*—” Damien held up a glass of blended fruit and ice in salute “—and wait.”

“Or you could go back home and go to bed,

since I'm here now," she suggested. "George said you pulled thirty-six hours straight, so I think you need the sleep more than I do."

"I appreciate the offer, but I think I'll stay since I've been with Maria through this entire pregnancy. And she did ask me, specifically, if I would check the baby after it's born." He held his *refresco* out to her. "Papaya and passion fruit. Really good. Want a sip?"

What she wanted was to go deliver a baby, but seeing as how that wasn't going to happen, she still wanted to get into Maria's bedroom and watch what was going on. Hitching her rucksack higher onto her shoulder, she passed by Damien, whose feet were now propped up on the chair opposite him, and headed on back through the kitchen. "I'll let you know if it's a boy or girl," she said before she stepped into the back hall.

"It's a boy," he called after her.

"You did some testing to find out?" Juliette asked, clearly surprised that he'd go to such lengths for someone who wanted as little medical intervention as possible.

"No tests. Just a guess. And I'm usually pretty

good at guessing. Got my last five deliveries right. No reason to break that winning streak now."

"You're that confident, are you?"

In answer, he picked up his *refresco*, took a sip, then said, "Yep!"

Damn, he was sexy, sitting there in all his casual, cocky glory. She really didn't want to think that of him, and maybe her guard was let down because she was so tired but, God help her, she was beginning to like Damien. Not enough to fall for him, in spite of his somewhat unusual charm, but enough to tolerate his ways.

"Can I come in?" she asked, pushing open Maria's bedroom door.

The women in the room all turned to look at her—all but the oldest one, who was seated at the end of the bed, obviously ready to deliver a baby. "Who are you?" one of the women asked.

"Juliette Allen. El doctor Juliette Allen."

"No doctor needed here," the woman at the end of the bed said quite sternly.

"That's what el doctor Damien told me, so I'm not here as a doctor. I'm just here to watch. And if you need someone else to help…"

"Irene needs no help," another one of the women informed her.

Juliette sighed. If Damien were here, he'd be enjoying this rejection. "I won't get in the way."

"Don't get in the way somewhere else," Irene, Maria's grandmother, said. "Maria doesn't need a stranger here."

Struggling to be patient, Juliette smiled, and backed her way over to the door, where she stopped and simply stood, without saying another word. Apparently that was good enough for the women, as they turned their attention back to Maria, who was bearing down in a hard push.

"Push harder," Irene encouraged her.

"I can't," the pregnant woman moaned. "Can't push. Can't…breathe. Getting too tired."

When Juliette heard this, she was instantly on alert. "Maybe reposition her," she suggested. "Get her head up a little higher. More like she's sitting rather than laying."

Her suggestion was greeted with frowns from everyone in the room. "My grandmother knows how high she's supposed to sit," one of the younger women said, her voice curt.

Before Juliette could respond, a scream from

Maria ripped through the room. "I can't do this!" she cried. "The baby's not coming."

This was more than Juliette could take, and she pushed her way through the crowd in the room and went straight to Irene's side to bend down and take a look. But what she saw was no progression toward birth. No crowning whatsoever. "How long has she been in heavy labor?" Juliette asked the woman.

"Not long enough," the woman responded belligerently.

"I *mean* in hours. How long in hours?"

"About one," one of the women called out.

"And it's been heavy like this since the beginning?" Contractions coming almost one after another.

"She always has her babies fast," Irene conceded. "But I think this one is taking too long. I'm worried I don't see the baby's head yet."

"Can I take a look?" Juliette asked, slinging her rucksack down onto the floor, then opening it up to grab out a blood pressure cuff. Damn, she wished she was back in her clinic, where she could hook up a fetal monitor, because her greatest fear right now was that the baby was in distress and she had no way to observe it.

"Maria's having trouble. So if you could move over and let me get a look at her…"

Irene hesitated for a moment, then nodded and moved aside. "You can help her?"

"I'm going to try," Juliette said, taking her position at the end of the bed. "Could you hold back the sheets for me, so I've got a little more room to maneuver?" It wasn't really necessary, but she wanted to include Irene since she was such a vital part of childbirth here in Bombacopsis, and all the women in the village respected her. There was no way Juliette wanted to dismiss Irene and diminish her in the eyes of all the people who trusted her. "And also make sure Maria stays in position?"

Irene agreed readily, and moved into her place next to Juliette, where she did everything Juliette asked.

"It's good we have you here," the old woman finally said, after Juliette had completed her initial exam. "El doctor Damien is good enough, but this should be left up to a woman."

Juliette smiled, hoping that this might be the beginning of the village accepting something they'd never before seen—a female doctor.

"Did I hear my name mentioned?" Damien asked, poking his head through the door.

"Just in that the ladies here believe this is no place for a man," Juliette returned. Then continued, "But I do need some help, in spite of that."

"What's going on?" he asked, stepping fully into the room.

"We have an obstructed labor in progress," Juliette called over the increasing noise of the women surrounding her. "In spite of Maria's strong contractions, her labor isn't progressing."

Juliette pumped up her blood pressure cuff and tried to hear the dull thudding of Maria's heartbeat after she placed the bell of her stethoscope underneath the cuff. "Her blood pressure is high," she called out. "As best as I can tell." Then she felt Maria's belly, pressed down on it to determine the position of the baby. "Baby's in normal position. But not progressing down the birth canal."

"She needs to push again," Irene shouted over the crowd.

"Pushing's not going to help now," Juliette explained. "The baby's ready to come. But it's not, and trying to push now is only going to make things worse. Put the baby at some risk."

The noise of the women was growing louder, deafening, fraying Juliette's already frayed nerves. Maria was in trouble, she needed Damien to help her with this and she couldn't even communicate with him, the ladies were so loud. Pressure mounting. Maria moaning even louder. Ladies getting frantic. More pressure—

"Damien!" she finally yelled. "Can we get these people out of here? I can't do what I need to do with everybody hovering over me, shouting the way they are." She was trying her best to shut out all the confusion going on around her, but alarm for Maria's lack of pushing out the baby was making everybody crazy, including her. "We've got a problem going on, and I can't do what I need to do with everyone hovering over me." Her own anxiety for Maria and her baby was increasing.

"Give me a couple of seconds," Damien called back to her.

She couldn't see him, as the door was at such an angle it wasn't in her line of sight. But she felt reassured just having him in the room. She felt even more reassured when each of the women started to leave the room. Whatever Damien was saying to them was working, and she was glad for that as Maria had turned a pasty white and was slowly sinking into total exhaustion.

"What have we got?" Damien asked, once all the ladies, with the exception of Irene, had exited.

"Nothing. Absolutely nothing."

"Her contractions?" Damien approached the bed and took Maria's pulse.

"Strong and almost continuous. The baby should be coming out now, and I'm getting worried that it's not."

He nodded, and immediately tore into the rucksack he was carrying, producing, in just a matter of seconds, a scalpel, a sterile drape, forceps and a handheld suction device. "Six minutes," he said, as he grabbed a bottle of sterile wash and pulled the sheet off Maria's belly.

"What?" Juliette asked him.

"I can do an emergency C-section in six minutes from the time I get her sedated. Faster, if I have to. So, stand on the opposite side of me, and let's get this thing done." Then, to Maria, "Maria! Can you hear me? It's el doctor Damien, and I'm going to get your baby out of you right now. But

I'm going to have to make a little cut in your belly to do so." He looked over at Juliette. "How long will it take you to get an IV going?"

"Not long," she said, immediately plowing through her medical rucksack to find the necessary equipment. Tubing, needle, IV drip solution. "What are we going to put in it?"

"I've got ketamine."

"Ketamine?" she asked. "You didn't mention that in your drug list."

"Because it's hard for me to come by and I put the little bit I do have back for emergencies."

Resourceful, she thought. Ketamine was a valuable property. "Well, a low-dose application of ketamine will work, since this baby's going to be out of her before the ketamine can cross the blood barrier," she said, as she readied to stick the IV catheter in Maria's arm. In no time at all, the IV was started, and Juliette handed Irene the bag of drip solution to hold above the head of the bed so the medication would run down into Maria's vein, while she piggy-backed on a pouch of ketamine. As soon as the medications were both in place, Juliette opened up the port to let them pass through the tubing into Maria's body. It took only a couple of minutes for the anesthetization of Maria Salas to commence. "Ready?" she finally asked Damien, noting that he'd prepped the incision site whilst she started the IV.

"Put a clock on it," he said, poised to make the first incision through Maria's abdomen.

Juliette did, and Damien was right. Six minutes and ten seconds into the procedure and he was handing over a brand-new baby for her to check. "A boy," she said.

"I was right," Damien said, grinning. "And he's a big one. I'm guessing nine or ten pounds."

"Closer to ten," Juliette said, as she turned her attention to baby Salas while Damien finished up with Maria. First she did the normal suctioning—mouth, nose. Then she took a towel and wrapped it around the baby, poking him gently, trying to get him to cry.

"Is he OK?" Damien asked, looking over at Juliette for a moment.

"Well, I don't have any equipment to do a proper evaluation, but he's breathing and his heart is beating."

"But he's not crying?" Damien asked.

"Not yet."

"Pinch him gently. Just a little one to see what you get." Damien grabbed up a pre-threaded suture and began to stitch up Maria's incision. But he took a second to look over at Juliette as she gave the baby a slight tweak on the bottom of his left foot. And got no response.

So she switched to tickling. Tickled a little spot on the baby's upper arm and ran her fingers down his arm lightly to his wrist, then waited for a second when he didn't respond, and tried it again. This time, baby Salas sucked in a lungful of air and let out with a royal scream.

"Good work," Damien said, without looking up at Juliette.

"How's Maria?"

"Hanging in there."

"Want me to finish closing for you?" she asked, handing the baby over to Manuela—Maria's sister—who'd snuck back into the room to be by her sister's side.

"No, I'm good. But what you can do is go outside and tell someone in the yard to run over to the hospital and fetch a stretcher. Then round up some volunteers to carry Maria over once I get through here."

"You OK?" Juliette asked before she left the room.

He finally looked up at Juliette, his brown eyes twinkling and his smile spreading from ear to ear. "I just delivered a baby. That always makes me OK."

"We do good work together," Damien commented as he and Juliette walked back to the hospital, arm in arm in the dark, leaning heavily on one another. He was tired. Almost too tired to function. But Maria and the baby were probably being settled into the hospital by now, so he had to take one more look at them before he dragged himself back to his hut for what was left of the night.

"It was a pretty slick delivery," Juliette admitted. "My first C-section since I assisted in one during my residency. Then later, in *my* clinic, I referred all my pregnancies to the obstetrics department."

"Well, around here you get to do it all. Bandage a stubbed toe, remove an infected appendix, treat malaria, remedy a bad heartburn. You know, jack-of-all-trades."

"So, I know you're a surgeon, but did you learn

these other things in your training, or do you just learn as you go?"

Truthfully, it had been a culture shock coming here. No matter where he'd worked prior to this, he'd always surrounded himself with a security blanket in that he'd kept strictly to his general surgery, never wandering very far from it. Then this, where he had to wander in all different directions.

"It's been a huge learning curve. And yeah, a lot of it I do make up as I go. But the people here are patient with me."

"Do you consult outsiders? You know, friends or colleagues from your old days?"

"Not so much. We don't have great access to the outside world. Although, if I need to know something bad enough, I'll go into Cima de la Montaña and scare up an internet connection." They walked on by his hut, where he took a wistful glance at the front door, wishing he was back in there right now, sleeping peacefully in his uncomfortable bed. "And I did have several of my medical references shipped down to me, so I've always got those to fall back on, even though they're pretty outdated."

"Well, if there's ever anything you want me to look up for you, let me know and I'll do it when I go back to San José, then I'll get the answer back to you next time I come."

"Are you really coming back?" he asked her. "I mean, your first day has been pretty tough so far, and I haven't exactly been welcoming." That was putting it mildly. He'd been downright awful, which he regretted as Juliette was a real trooper. She'd come here first thing this morning, pitched right in and done everything that needed to be done. More, actually. She'd spotted the problem in Maria's labor, and the way she had assisted with the C-section was downright amazing!

"Have you been trying to get rid of me? Is that why you've been so rude? Because I thought you needed someone else here."

They entered the hospital where, down the hall in the ward, George Perkins was settling Maria Salas into bed. Irene, her grandmother, had seated herself in a chair next to the bed and was holding the baby. Maria's husband, Alvaro, was standing at the foot of the bed along with five other people Damien assumed were relatives or close friends.

"I do need someone here. I just wasn't expecting...you."

"What were you expecting?" she asked him.

"I'm not sure, really. Maybe someone close to retirement age, or someone's who's basically burned out the way George was. The thing is, when you have very little to offer, you can't expect your pick of the profession to come knocking on your door. Then when you showed up here—well, you're closer to the pick of the profession, and I simply didn't expect that. It caught me off guard. Gave me some hope I'm probably not entitled to have."

"So you immediately turned rude, because you didn't think you deserved someone like me, with my background and skills?"

"I immediately turned defensive, because I thought there was no way in hell I'd get to keep you here after you'd seen what I had to offer." It was too late, he was too tired. Otherwise, he wouldn't be standing here confessing to things that were true but would otherwise never be admitted to. In the course of one day, Juliette had softened him. Whether that was a good thing remained to be seen.

Time would tell, he supposed. "Before we go look at Maria, would you care for a cup of hot tea? Herbal, so it won't keep you awake."

"Want me to make it?" she asked him.

Damien shook his head. "A cup of tea is the least I can do for you. Oh, and Juliette, how about you take my hut for the rest of the night so you can get some sleep? I think it's going to be pretty busy, and pretty noisy, in here."

"But you need sleep worse than I do."

"I've got my exam table."

"Which is ungodly uncomfortable. No, you go back to your hut and I'll stay here."

"And here, I'm trying to be nice to you."

Juliette shook her head, then smiled. "Don't be too nice, because if you are I'm afraid I won't recognize you."

And that was the problem. He wanted her to recognize him.

CHAPTER FIVE

"IT WAS BUSY," Juliette said to Cynthia over a typical Costa Rican breakfast called *gallo pinto*, made of black beans and rice. Some restaurants made it with bacon, eggs, ham and a number of other ingredients, but Juliette preferred hers plain, as her appetite was never large in the morning. "A lot of people come in with general complaints, and that takes up most of the time. So I saw gout, bug bites, a broken finger—those kinds of things. But I also assisted in an emergency C-section, which was a good opportunity for me to learn since all my pregnant ladies at the hospital back in Indiana got referred to the obstetrics clinic."

Cynthia snapped her head up and looked across the table at Juliette. "You did a C-section? How? Because what I've been gathering is that your little hospital isn't equipped to do much of anything."

"It's not. But that didn't matter, because we did

it at the patient's home." She took a sip of coffee then sat the mug back down on the table. This had become her morning routine.

A small portion of *gallo pinto* and coffee in the tiny little restaurant down the block from her flat. It was cheap, filling, and once she'd gotten used to the starchy heaviness that early in the day, she'd actually grown to like the concoction.

"It was a little dicey, since I've never assisted in a C-section outside my residency, but Damien was there and he's a skilled surgeon so Maria—the patient—was in good hands."

"Is he cute?"

"Who?"

"Damien. What's he look like? Tall, dark and handsome? Great body? Nice smile? Soft hands?"

"Whoa," Juliette said, thrusting out her hand to stop her friend. "I was too busy working to pay *that* kind of attention to him." Nice words, not exactly true, however, as she *had* paid a little attention to him. And while Damien wasn't the physical type she'd always been attracted to, something about his blatant rawness was appealing. Sexy. "Actually, he *is* tall, dark and handsome. I did notice that much." With drop-dead gorgeous brown eyes, and a beautiful smile punctuated by the most appealing dimples she'd ever seen on a man. "And I have an idea that in his real surroundings, he's probably a bad boy."

Cynthia's eyes lit up. "Maybe I'll have to go out there with you sometime. I *really* like bad boys."

"He'll put you to work," Juliette warned. "Make you change beds."

"As long as *his* bed is included in that, I won't mind."

It almost put Juliette off, seeing how her friend was reacting to a man she'd never met, let alone seen.

"He's grumpy."

"So?"

"I mean, *really* grumpy."

"Yeah, but there are ways to soothe the savage beast."

"Aren't you engaged or something?"

A dreamy look overtook Cynthia's eyes. "To my one and only. But a girl can still look, can't she?"

Actually, Juliette didn't know since she'd never been one who was much into looking. Something else always got in the way, always took up her time and energy.

"Look, I need to get on into work. I've got a prospective GI doc coming in about half an hour, and I want to take him over to the hospital and show him around, so he'll have time to acquaint himself with the facility before his interview." She also just needed to get away from Cynthia for a little, to clear her head. To put some proper perspective on why she felt the way she did where Damien was concerned. "So why don't you finish up here, and I'll see you when you get to work."

"Do you have a thing for him, Juliette?" Cynthia asked bluntly.

"A thing?" There was no *thing* going on with her—except maybe a smidge of fascination. And that didn't qualify as a *thing*, did it?

"You know—something going on. Or maybe just a feeling. Because I think you're mad at me right now because I teased you about him."

Cynthia's reaction to Damien might have been teasing but, for a reason Juliette didn't understand, it had struck a raw nerve in her. "I'm not mad at you, and I don't have a *thing* with, or for, Damien." Said a little too vehemently, she was afraid. Which she was sure Cynthia would misinterpret.

"Well, I was just joking with you. I mean, I've got Carlos and I'm not looking to get involved with anyone else. Not even your Damien."

"He's not *my* Damien, and I'm not looking to get involved with him, either."

"Then you two didn't hit it off?"

Juliette shook her head. "He's a talented doctor, which I respect, but apart from that…" She shrugged. "He's just not my type." A sentiment that wasn't necessarily true, if she took into account all the many times she'd thought about him since she'd come back to San José just this morning. "Besides, I don't have time for a personal life. Between my two jobs, I barely have time to sleep."

"And whose fault is that? Aren't you the one who works the late hours and, as often as not, goes in early? And aren't you the one who always goes out of her way to help clients in ways not required of our job?"

What Cynthia said was true. But, in her own defense, these were the things she did to make sure the people who were trusting her to make a perfect medical match for them got everything they hoped for. She took her job seriously—as seriously as Damien took his job in his impoverished little jungle hospital. As seriously as her dad took his job in a large, university teaching hospital. "I'm just doing the best I can."

"And not enjoying your life while you're doing it. You're going to get tired of living that way, Juliette," Cynthia warned. "When I first came here, I was just like you—too dedicated. It almost burned me out. But eventually I began to back away from it and find a life outside of my work."

"You fell in love with a doctor at one of the hospitals," Juliette replied, smiling. "That'll give you a new life."

"If you let it. And, from what I can see of you, you're not letting it."

"I've barely been here a month, Cynthia. I hardly know my way around my desk yet."

"Well, keep your mind open to this jungle doctor. Your eyes lit up when you mentioned him." Cynthia shoved back from the little table for two and stood. "In the meantime, I think I'll go in a little early with you, and give Carlos a call."

"Didn't he just leave the flat like two hours ago?"

"Maybe he did, but I miss him already."

"Spoken like a woman in love," she said to Cynthia.

Of course, for Juliette, love was only an idea, a notion. Something that sounded beautiful. But she'd never been in love. Never pictured herself as someone who was lovable, as no one had ever fallen in love with her. Of course she wasn't sure she'd ever given anyone the chance. She'd been too busy, between her work and her father. In some ways, she was turning into him—always striving to take on more work, then hiding behind it in lieu of a real life. Building block upon block, which turned into a fortress. Well, she was finding herself more and more cloistered inside that fortress every day, wanting to get out of it. And Costa Rica was her out. Falling in love with someone, though, was the best out she could think of. But she didn't know if that would happen.

"Well, just give it time," Cynthia said. "Maybe you'll find the love of your life here, in Costa Rica, too."

Wishful thinking as she didn't know where to look for it. She was too inexperienced when it came to love. Embarrassed by the fact that, at thirty-three, she didn't know a thing about it. Saddened by the fact that she might have let it pass her by without even seeing it.

"Quit looking at the road, Damien," George Perkins said as he was changing a bandage on Alfonso Valverde, the local mechanic. He'd been working on a truck manifold and received a nasty burn, which he hadn't treated at the time. Now it was infected and the infection had spread from his thumb to his entire hand. "She'll get here when she gets here."

"I expected her an hour ago," Damien said, fighting to keep his eyes off the front window.

"Maybe she had car trouble. Or got swallowed up in one of the potholes on the way out here. Or maybe a jaguar…" George grinned up at Damien. "Or maybe she's just late."

"Or decided she didn't want to come."

"Without getting word to you?" George shook his head. "She doesn't seem the type. Of course, I really don't know what type she is, so maybe I'm not the one who should be telling you to quit looking."

Fat lot of help that was! He'd spent the whole week thinking about Juliette, planning on ways to make this weekend better for her. Of course, he'd also spent the week reminding himself of all the reasons he didn't want to get involved with a rich girl again. And he stretched that involvement to include working with her.

"Well, I'm going to run down the street and see Padre Benicio. He hasn't been feeling well for the last couple of days and since he refuses to come into the hospital, the hospital's going to him."

"Tell him for me that Carmelita and I want to get married in a few weeks, so he'd better get over what's ailing him, because I don't want a sick priest anywhere near me on my wedding day."

"It's allergies," Damien said. "He's not contagious."

"Well, I don't want him sneezing his allergies all over my bride."

"You're actually going to go through with it?"

George taped the end of the bandage and put on his reading glasses to make a close inspection of his work. "I'm almost sixty, so why wait? She's given me a second chance at life."

"Well, I wish you and Carmelita the best of luck. And, for what it's worth, I think you're a great couple. She's good for you." The man had so much faith in the power of love it almost made Damien want to believe again.

"Sorry I'm late," Juliette called from the doorway. "I didn't get away from San José as early as I'd hoped to."

Without turning to face her, Damien said, "You're late? I didn't notice."

George shook his head, rolled his eyes and gave Damien a pat on the shoulder as he walked out the door. "Good luck with Damien," he said to Juliette. "He's in a mood tonight."

"Another mood?" Juliette asked.

"My mood's no better or worse than it ever is," Damien replied, slinging his medical rucksack over his shoulder.

"Something I've looked forward to all week," Juliette replied. "So, are you going out on a house call?"

"I am. And George's off tonight, so the hospital is all yours for now."

"But you're coming back, aren't you?"

"Eventually." Actually, he wanted to get back as quickly as he could, but that would make him seem anxious, maybe even desperate. So, to avoid anything that made him look the least bit interested in Juliette, he decided to take the long road home, stop at the village café for a bite to eat—he had a taste tonight for *arreglados*, a tiny sandwich filled with meat and salad—then afterward he might wander on over to see how Javier Rojas was responding to the new medication he'd prescribed for him: cyclobenzaprine, a drug used for treating the muscle spasms he was having in his back. Anything to keep him away for a while. Anything to give him time to think about some unexpected feelings he was having. Unexpected, and quick, as he'd known her only a week.

"And if I need help while you're gone?"

"Alegria's on tonight. Right now she's gathering up the hospital gowns from the lady who washes them for us, but she should be back here in about fifteen minutes."

Damn! This wasn't the way he'd envisioned the evening starting out. Every single day this past week he'd come up with a new scenario. He and Juliette would pitch in together and check every patient in the hospital. He and Juliette would have a nice meal together before they started work. He and Juliette would simply sit down together and have a pleasant chat. The list of scenarios went on and on, yet here he was, leaving her all alone. No *he and Juliette* anything!

"So you want me to make beds again?"

"Actually, what I'd like is for you to make a bedside check of all the patients. You know, get their vital signs, assess them for whatever we're treating them for, address wounds, that sort of thing. Oh, and we've got seven patients admitted right now. Nothing seriously wrong with any of them, so you shouldn't have a tough evening."

"How's Maria Salas and her baby doing?"

"Maria's doing fine. So is Alejandro, her baby. We sent them home day before yesterday, and she's due back in here tomorrow so we can make sure nothing's going wrong with her incision." He paused, and frowned. "You know, to save her the trip over here, I might just stop by her house this evening to take a look." At the rate he was going, he'd be lucky to get back to the hospital by midnight.

"Well, it looks like I've got a busy night ahead of me. Guess I should get to work." Instead of heading into the hospital ward, though, she turned and started walking toward the clinic.

"Where are you going?" Damien asked her.

"I ran into Padre Benicio on the way in. He's got a terrible cough, and he said he's coming down with a sore throat now. So I'm going to go take a look at him. He's in the clinic right now, waiting for me."

"How'd you get him here when I've been trying for days, and he's refused me every time?"

"Simple. I asked." Juliette smiled, and shrugged. "What can I say? I have good powers of persuasion."

"That's all it took?"

"Well, that, and I also promised to pick up a book for him when I get back to San José."

"So, you're bribing a priest. Guess I never thought of that."

"Actually I didn't either, but he laid the opportunity out there by mentioning a book he'd like to have, and I grabbed it."

"Well, your new *bribed* friend has allergies," Damien said, chuckling. "He's allergic to the flowers on the trumpet tree. They produce these lovely white flowers that go perfectly with a bat's nocturnal activities. The flower is closed up during the day and opens only at night, revealing its pollen-releasing stamen, which attracts the bats. Padre Benicio is allergic to the pollen."

"You had him tested for that?"

Damien shook his head. "Nope. Just applied common sense. He's improved during the day, pretty much to the point that he functions normally. But at night all hell breaks loose with his allergies. Which means that it's related to something that comes up every night. The trumpet trees are blooming right now, and since that happens at night—" He shrugged. "Common sense."

"Ah, yes, the standard at El Hospital Bombacopsis."

"Hey, it works! When you don't have the proper equipment at your disposal, you learn to rely on your own instincts or gut reactions."

"If you trust yourself that much."

Juliette was a confident woman. Somehow, he didn't see her as someone who wouldn't trust herself.

"It's a class they should probably offer in medical school, because there are a lot of doctors, all over the world, who are treating by the seat of their pants, the way we do here."

"Well, Padre Benicio is a lucky man since his

diagnosis does make common sense. Like Señor Mendez and his gout."

Damien nodded. "We do the best we can with what we've got."

"And, apparently, you've got a good gut instinct. Anyway, how are you treating Padre Benicio?"

"Diphenhydramine."

"That's it? Something over the counter?"

"It's all I have on hand, and I wouldn't have even had that if not for the generosity of someone who passed through the village a month ago and left their bottle of it behind. Unopened, and well in advance of its expiration date, in case you're interested."

"Is it working?"

Damien shook his head. "Nope. Which is why Padre Benicio calls me over to the rectory every couple of nights. He keeps hoping we've got some relief for him."

"Which you don't." Juliette frowned. "Damien, you can't just let him go untreated, especially if he's really suffering from this. And, judging from what I saw of him outside, he is."

"I'm not going to let him go untreated. In fact, I'm going into Cima de la Montaña sometime this week, and when I'm there I'll get on a computer and order something that might work better for him. Maybe a steroidal nasal spray and an inhaler for his wheezing."

"How long will that take?"

"After I get it ordered, it'll probably take a week or so to get it to Cima de la Montaña, then another few days for me to go pick it up. So probably going on two weeks, total."

"That's too long. Let me pick up something in San José when I go back, and bring it with me next week. That'll shave off a week, which isn't great, but it's better than him having to wait for two."

She'd bring it back with her? Meaning she was coming back again? That gave Damien another week to get it right with Juliette. Another week to fret over how he was going to do that.

"Your gout is acting up again, Señor Mendez?" Juliette showed him into the clinic and pointed to the exam table. "Go ahead and have a seat, then take your shoe and sock off." Once again, the man didn't seem quite right, and her first inclination was to ask him about it. But she thought back to what Damien had said about treating the patients as they came. That was the hospital policy, so she'd follow it.

"Hurting bad tonight. I thought you could give me something for the pain so I can sleep better."

"You're not sleeping well?"

"My legs shake. They keep me up."

She wasn't getting a good feeling about this. "Can you take your trousers down so I can look at your legs?"

"Could el doctor Damien look at my legs?" the man asked.

"He's not going to be back for a while."

"I can wait," Señor Mendez said.

But *she* couldn't. She'd been on duty two hours already, and still hadn't gotten around to doing a general patient assessment. And there were other things that had to be attended to, so a shy patient was the last thing she needed right now.

"Maybe I can just rest on this table. It would feel good on my back."

"Your back hurts, too?" That plus the fact that his speech was definitely slurred tonight.

"Sometimes when I get tired. But it goes away after I rest."

"Do you ever feel any tingling in your face, or arms, or legs?" This was sounding even worse.

"Yes, but it always goes away."

"Do you get dizzy?"

"When I stand up too fast. Sometimes when I stand in one place too long."

Alarm was beginning to prickle up her spine. "I really need for you to take your trousers down. Just your trousers, nothing else." If she'd made an error in diagnosing him the first time, she wanted to be the one to correct it. "This will only take a minute."

Reluctantly, Señor Mendez slid off the end of the exam table, unfastened his belt and let his trousers drop to the floor. Juliette noticed that the man was staring intently at the ceiling. "Can you get back up on the table now?"

Exhaling a heavy sigh, Señor Mendez crawled back up on the table, and still stared upward. He clearly didn't like being in this position in front of a woman.

"I'm going to poke you in the leg, in several places, and I want you to tell me if what you feel is sharp or dull." She pulled a probe from a supply drawer and went to work. "OK, sharp or dull?"

she asked, taking her first poke at the man's leg. When he responded that it felt dull, she went onto another site, then another and another, until she was pretty well convinced that he had an overall numbness in both legs. "You can pull up your trousers now," she said, as she dropped the probe back into the drawer, feeling totally discouraged by what she suspected.

"Am I sick?" he asked her.

"Do you smoke ganja?"

"No. Never."

Too bad he didn't, because she was now hoping he did. That would have been an easy diagnosis. This, unfortunately, wasn't going to be easy. "Do you still work?"

"Every day. I work on a farm, tending the cows. Sometimes I go to pick coffee beans."

"And the tingling you get, or your occasional dizziness, does that ever stop that?"

"No. I work hard every day. But it tires me out now that I'm getting older."

"How old are you?" she asked.

"Thirty."

Younger than her! All the other symptoms, plus gout—meaning compromised immune system—

Juliette felt as if she'd just swallowed a heavy lump of dough that had plunked right down in the bottom of her stomach. "Look, I'm going to give you some ibuprofen for the pain." From the bottles she'd brought to donate to the drug supply. "That should help you tonight, but I want you to come back to the hospital tomorrow. Will you do that?"

"Early, *señorita*. Before I go to work."

"That's fine. I'll be here, and el doctor Damien should be back by then." She hoped.

Actually, it was two hours later when el doctor Damien finally wandered through the door. "Anything happen while I was out?" he asked, heading straight into the exam room and dropping down onto the exam table, laying back and cupping his hands under his head.

"Señor Mendez came in for his gout again."

"What did you do for him?"

"Gave him ibuprofen and sent him home."

"We have ibuprofen now?"

"Ibuprofen and another supply of penicillin. One of my hospitals donated it to me."

"Then you come with some advantages. I'm impressed."

"Well, if a few drugs impresses you, prepare yourself to be wowed, as I also come with a new diagnosis for Señor Mendez."

Damien frowned. "He doesn't have gout?"

"Oh, he has gout, all right. But he's thirty years old, Damien. Remember when we talked over our concern about him being too young for it?"

"Absolutely. But he denied having anything wrong with him when I did his physical. So with this gout—there's nothing else we can do except treat him for what he presented with. And hope that if he does start having other symptoms he'd tell us." He paused for a moment, then frowned. "Are there other symptoms now?"

"Now, and probably for quite some time. He has dizzy spells. His legs are marginally numb. He has slurred speech—the slurred speech I attributed to marijuana use. He gets tired too easily for someone his age, and his legs get too jerky for him to sleep."

Damien sat up and sighed heavily. "Damn," he muttered. "He never mentioned any of this. Not a word of it."

"My sentiments, too," she said, clearly frustrated by the situation.

"Well, we've got to take care of it," Damien said. "And I sure as hell don't know how we're going to go about it, since this isn't going to get fixed with a gut reaction and a penicillin pill. Any suggestions?"

"We need to get him into a hospital in San José, and I'm not going to be the one to convince him to do it. The man didn't even want to drop his trousers for me to take a look at his legs."

"Then I'll just tell him he has to go."

"And get him there, how?"

"Any number of the villagers will loan me a truck or a car."

"You mean you'd drive him in yourself?"

"I made the original mistake, didn't I?"

"It's not a mistake when a patient holds something back. We're only human, Damien. We can only see so much. And when a patient doesn't tell you what to look for, doesn't tell you what else is going wrong with him, how can you be expected to diagnose him with multiple sclerosis, or anything else, for that matter?"

"But he told you."

"I had to pry it out of him. But I'm used to prying it out of patients. That's a good bit of what a family practice is about. As a surgeon, you don't have to do that prying. The diagnosis has already been made by the time the patient reaches you, and all you have to do is patch, fix or remove something. So don't beat yourself up over this, because it was his choice not to disclose."

"Ugly diagnosis, all the same," Damien said, sliding off the exam table. "And how the hell am I supposed to treat that condition out here?"

"There are drugs..."

"Which no one can afford."

"And there are therapies we could do right here to treat some of the underlying dysfunctions that will occur. You know, exercises for cognition, various disciplines for weakness, those sorts of things."

"None of which I'm qualified to do."

"Come on, Damien. I'm trying to look on the bright side here. Señor Mendez isn't without hope."

"Hope comes in the form of convenience, Juliette. Which we're fresh out of here."

"So what do you want to do? Just sit back and watch him deteriorate because there's no hope? Oh, and feel sorry for yourself in the process because you have limitations?" She knew how he was feeling, as she was feeling the very same way. But this hospital needed Damien to function normally and, right now, she was the only one who could snap him out of his frustration.

"I don't feel sorry for myself."

"Then you're angry with yourself."

"Don't I have a right to be?"

"Damien, you chose to work in a very limited hospital. You knew, coming in, that you wouldn't have any kind of modern medicine at your disposal, yet you stayed here because you wanted to help. Give yourself some credit for that. Most doctors would have walked away because it was too difficult. But you stayed, and you do make a difference."

"Couldn't prove it right now."

"You know what? We need to pick up from right here and move forward, because that's what Señor Mendez needs us to do. No matter how he was diagnosed prior to this, and no matter how he'll be diagnosed after this, he's got a tough life ahead of him and you and George and I are the only ones who are going to get him through it."

"You say that like you intend on being in it for the long haul."

"Honestly, I don't know what I intend for my own personal long haul, but I'm in it right now and I intend on doing everything I can to help my patient. Which includes making arrangements at one of the hospitals for all the proper tests to be done. So, how are we going to accomplish that?"

Damien ran a frustrated hand through his hair. "You make the hospital arrangements this week and I'll bring him into San José next Friday, drop him off for the weekend to have his tests. Then I'll pick you up and bring you back to Bombacopsis to save you the drive, and take you back to San José Monday morning, when I go to fetch Señor Mendez."

Juliette was relieved that Damien was finally beginning to turn his inward guilt into the outward process that would accomplish what Señor Mendez needed. She appreciated the effort it took to do that.

"Look, Damien. Neither of us has really made a mistake yet. Señor Mendez is in early symptoms, and his condition might well have gone unnoticed for years. What we did was just treat what we saw, which is, really, all we can do when we don't have the proper facilities to do anything more. I feel horrible that I mistook his symptoms for drug use, but I can't let that stop me from moving forward with a different treatment. And you can't let it stop you because all you saw was gout. You diagnosed that properly."

"And you went from there and diagnosed multiple sclerosis."

"Because, in my specialty, I have to connect the dots. I look at a broad spectrum of symptoms to figure out what's going on. Relate one thing to another until I get it worked out. As a surgeon, you don't do that so much. You fix the specific thing you were called on to fix."

"But I'm not a surgeon here."

"Sure you are. Once a surgeon, always a surgeon. You were trained to think like a surgeon, and you were trained to act like a surgeon. That's what saved Maria Salas and her baby last week."

"Why are you trying so hard to cheer me up?"

"Because I have something else to tell you. Something you're not going to like. And I wanted to soften the blow."

He frowned. "What?"

"I didn't get around to doing patient assessments. I've been too busy." She knew it really wasn't a big deal, but she hoped her little distraction from Señor Mendez would defuse the moment.

"That's it?" His face melted into a smile. "You're confessing that you didn't follow my orders?"

"Something like that."

"Should I fire you?" he asked.

"That's an option. Or you could go help me do it now."

Damien laughed. "In spite of my bad mood and your naïveté, we're pretty good together, aren't we?" He stepped toward her, reached out and stroked her cheek, then simply stared at her for a moment. A long stare. A deep stare.

For an instant she thought he might kiss her and, for that same instant, she thought she might want him to. But he didn't. He simply smiled, stepped back, then walked away. And she was left wondering where a kiss might have taken them.

CHAPTER SIX

"NICE OFFICE," DAMIEN SAID, twisting around to see Juliette's entire suite. It was in a newer building, in a posh neighborhood, surrounded by other posh buildings and, for a moment, he almost envied her all this civilization. But only for a moment. He'd bought into this kind of a trap once before, and learned his lesson the hard way. "And you're in charge?"

"Just the United States division. I have five people working directly for me, and the office has another couple of recruiters who have their own staff."

"I'm impressed. But you ran a family practice clinic in Indianapolis, so how does that translate into this?"

"It's where I got my administrative experience. I recruited doctors and other medical personnel to my clinic, and it was a large practice, with thirty-six doctors on staff, as well as the associated professionals needed to fill the other positions."

"Sounds like a big job."

"On top of my own practice, it was. But it was necessary to maintain the quality of the care we offered. The best care coming from the best professionals."

"So, does your position here entail a lot of paperwork?" Personally, he hated paperwork. Hated all those details that had nothing to do with the actual medicine he was practicing. Which was why his jungle hospital was turning out to be a nice relief. With the exception of charting patient notes, there was no other paperwork involved. No insurance claims to fill out, no requisitions or vouchers to deal with. No nothing. And it was nice. So nice, in fact, he wondered if he could ever go back to a proper hospital and deal with all the superfluous things outside the actual patient care.

"Paperwork!" She snorted a laugh. "About half my job is the paperwork."

"And you like that?"

"No. I hate it. But I have to do it."

So she was diligent in her job, in spite of hating part of it. That was an admirable quality, one he, himself, didn't possess.

You have a week of charting to catch up on, Damien. Fill out the correct requisitions, Dr. Caldwell. Did you forget to submit an insurance justification for the treatment you prescribed?

Yep, he sure did hate all that. "Which makes a jungle hospital seem all the more attractive."

"Who are you trying to convince?" she asked.

"Don't need to convince anybody but myself, and I'm already convinced."

"As in staying there forever?"

"I don't commit to forever. Not in anything. A couple years is about as far as I'll go." And that was a year longer than it used to be. Of course, he was getting older. Not quite so eager to pick up and move so often.

Damien walked over to a fish tank that encompassed one entire wall, and stared in at the emerald catfish, a particularly shy little creature that was trying its best to hide from him. "So, how often do you get out of here?" he asked, as he was already beginning to feel a little shut in by his surroundings, a condition, he expected, resulting from spending the past year in the wide-open spaces.

"Every day. Sometimes several times in a day, going back and forth between the various hospitals. The job keeps me on the move."

"And you like it?" He turned around to face Juliette, taking particular note of the feminine way in which she dressed—a long crinkly cotton skirt in tones of green, blue and purple topped by a gauzy white blouse. Nice look. One he wasn't used to seeing on her.

"Actually, I do. I wasn't sure about it at first, since it's so different from anything I've ever done. But once I got really involved in the work—All I'm doing is dealing with the means to provide outstanding patient care, Damien. It's really quite gratifying, especially when you get to see the results of your work the way I do."

"Meaning, you follow the people you place?"

"For a little while. To make sure they're the best fit for the job, to make sure they're adjusting to their new position."

"Then why work for me? I mean, it's a long drive, and you get no rewards for doing what you do. Wouldn't it have been easier to take a part-time position here, in San José, in one of the hospitals you work with?"

"I did try to find something here before I came to you, but nothing seemed to fit into my schedule. The hospitals all wanted more than a couple days a week from me, and several of them insisted I'd have to take calls. Which I can't do, since I have to deal with people at all hours of the day and night. Except weekends."

It seemed to Damien that Juliette's life worked out to be very tough, as she didn't have any personal time scheduled into it for herself.

"Anyway—I got Señor Mendez settled into the hospital, so I'm ready to head back to Bombacopsis anytime you're ready to leave."

"How's he doing?"

"Understandably frightened. But bearing up."

"Well, I've been talking to a couple of specialists here, and if he does come back with a multiple sclerosis diagnosis, I think there are some things we can do to treat him. It's a difficult outlook, but not an impossible one. By the way, I need to stop at one of the hospitals on our way out. Just for a few minutes. Do you mind?" She grabbed a knee-length white lab coat off the peg by the door, then slung her overnight bag over her shoulder. "I have a new recruit there, an ophthalmologist, and I want to stop by to see how she's doing."

"I can do that for you," Cynthia said, stepping into the office. Her eyes immediately went to Damien, and she opened them wide in frank appreciation. "And I'll bet you're Damien, aren't you?"

"Last time I checked," he said, extending his hand to her. "And you are?"

"Cynthia Jurgensen."

"Doctor extraordinaire," Juliette supplied.

"Well, Cynthia, it's nice to meet you. Do you and Juliette go way back?"

"We only just met when we came here. I preceded her by a while, then trained her."

"When you weren't busy swooning on the phone to Carlos," Juliette teased. Then explained to Damien, "Carlos Herrera—her fiancé."

"The cardiologist?" Damien asked.

Cynthia beamed with pride. "You know him?"

"Vaguely. I made a referral to him a few months back. Good man!"

"He's the reason Cynthia's going to stay permanently in Costa Rica." She shrugged. "What we do for love, eh?"

"And you wouldn't stay if you fell in love with someone here?" Damien asked Juliette.

"Would you?" she asked in return.

That was a good question. One he couldn't answer, as he didn't anticipate love anymore. If it happened, it happened. If it didn't, he wasn't going to worry about it. Past experience had taught him it took up too much time, and time was a commodity he simply didn't have enough of these days.

"Look, I think we need to get going. It's a long trip back to Bombacopsis, and if we need to stop at the hospital first…"

"I said I could do that," Cynthia interjected.

Juliette shook her head. "I really have to do this myself, since she's there on my recommendation."

"You just can't stay away from it, can you?" he asked, smiling.

"What?"

"The patient experience—which, I might add, implies that you're in the wrong position since for you it always goes back to the patient."

"Just like my father," she said, half under her

breath. This was something she didn't want in her life—another man trying to dominate her. Her father had always dominated, and it seemed as if Damien was trying to. But she'd finally resisted her father and, compared to him, Damien was a piece of cake. So let him bring it on. She was finally ready for it!

"Did you ever consider that your father might be right?"

"I like my job finding new medical talent, Damien. And I like the hours I put in at your hospital. The rest of it's none of your business." With all the newfound confidence she could muster, Juliette opened the office door and stepped into the hall. "So, are you coming, or would you rather stand there and think of even more ways to insult me?"

Damien chuckled as he followed Juliette into the hall. "So, have I gone and set you off even before we start out?"

"I can resist you, Damien Caldwell. Try anything you want, but I can resist you!"

Juliette threw her lab coat into the seat next to her, tilted her head back against the headrest and closed her eyes. "Finally done for the week," she said as Damien engaged the truck he'd borrowed and began the journey back to Bombacopsis. "And I think the people I've brought here are, overall, working out pretty well."

"You've got good instincts."

"Thank you," she said. "That's about the nicest thing you've ever said to me." She was starting out her weekend tired. It had been a long, grueling week—so many interviews to conduct, so many contacts to make, so much paperwork to do. Physically, her work hadn't been demanding. Not like what she was used to in her clinic back in Indianapolis. But she was exhausted, nonetheless. Probably just emotional fatigue, high heat, high humidity, she told herself as the noise of the cranky truck motor sputtered her to sleep.

"Juliette?"

She felt the gentle nudging on her arm, but resisted opening her eyes.

"I need to make a stop in Cima de la Montaña to see if I have any mail. Is that OK?"

Damien's voice was so soothing she simply wanted to melt into it. "That's fine," she mumbled.

"Then I want to make a house call. I have a

patient who has just moved there from Bombacopsis, and he wants me to check his daughter. It sounds like infected tonsils. It's going to be a little delay, so I wanted to make sure you're up to it."

"I'm fine, Damien," she said, twisting in her seat to face the direction from which his voice was coming, yet still refusing to open her eyes.

"You've been sleeping," he said.

"Not sleeping. Just—resting my eyes." Too bad she couldn't rest her head on his shoulder.

"Well, your eyes have been resting a good two hours now, and you were resting so hard I began to wonder if you were sleeping, or dead."

"Two hours?" Her eyes shot open at this. "Are you serious?"

"Two hours, soft snoring, occasional mumbling."

She never took naps. Never! No matter how tired she got. For her to nap the way she had wasn't a good thing, and to do it in front of Damien? "I don't snore!" she said, sitting up straight in the seat.

"OK, so maybe it wasn't snoring so much as it was moaning."

"And I don't moan in my sleep. Neither do I mumble!"

"Well, somebody in this truck was fully invested in sleep sounds and, since I've been driving, I hope to God that wasn't me. So, are you feeling better now?"

"I was feeling fine to begin with. Just a little tired. Crazy week…"

"We all have them," he said sympathetically.

"Why are you being so nice to me?" she asked. "It's not like you, which has got me worried."

"Actually, you're the one who has me worried."

"Why? Because I took a nap?"

"Napping is fine. Fitful napping is a symptom."

"It is if you're sick. But I'm not sick."

Damien stopped the truck in front of a tiny wood-sided house and opened the driver's-side door. "Look, we've still got another hour before we're back in Bombacopsis. You look like you've been hit by a freight train, so why don't you get yourself another hour's worth of sleep?"

"A freight train? You sure have mastered the art of flattery."

"OK, maybe not a freight train. But at least a donkey cart." He grinned in at her. "Is that better?"

Juliette leaned her head back against the headrest once again, and shut her eyes. "Go do what you have to do, Damien. And if it takes you very long, you should have enough time to come up with your next round of insults. Or do you already have them stored up for me?"

He chuckled. "You do bring out the best in me."

"Thank heavens it's the best, because I'd really hate to see the worst." She settled back into the seat with a little wriggle, then deliberately turned her face away from him. "Now, go away. Leave me alone."

"Sounds like a direct dismissal to me."

With that, Damien grabbed his medical bag from behind the seat, then shut the truck door. And suddenly the truck cab was quiet. Too quiet.

"Shoot," she said, opening her eyes, and twisting around to watch him walk up the dirt path to the house, where a very anxious woman stood on the porch, wringing her hands. "Double shoot."

Reaching behind her seat, she grabbed hold of her own medical bag, jumped out of the truck and followed Damien into the house. "I may look like a donkey cart hit me, but I'm all you've got. So, what do you want me to do?"

"I knew you couldn't resist," he said, grinning.

Of course she couldn't. Not Damien. Not patient care. And this was getting very frustrating.

"Her parents are going to bring Pabla in," Damien said, tossing a handful of mail onto the seat next to him. Letters from home, advertisements that had an uncanny way of finding him even in the jungle, a medical journal, a pharmaceutical catalog. All waiting for him in his local pickup box. "In fact, they'll probably beat us there."

"Isn't there a place here, in Cima de la Montaña, where she could have her tonsils removed?"

"There's a GP here, and he's actually pretty good. Young guy, with a lot of ideals. But he doesn't do surgery. So he sends his minor procedures over to me, and anything major into San José."

"Like you're set up to do even the minor procedures."

"We do the best we can. Dr. Villalobos, here in Cima de la Montaña. George and me—and even you—back in Bombacopsis. Also Frank Evigan, a chiropractor-turned-medic who practices out of a one-room hut about an hour and a half east of us. That's the real Costa Rica, Juliette, and it's nothing like the one you live in, where you have first-rate hospitals, normal medical amenities and highly trained doctors coming in from all over the world to be part of it."

"But you stick with it, in spite of the hardships."

"Somebody has to." And, for now, he was that appointed somebody. In truth, he was glad he was. After a year, he was rather fond of his little hospital in Bombacopsis, hardships and all.

"Do you ever want to go back to a surgical practice, Damien? In society—a big city?"

"At least twice a day. I loved what I did. Loved that my scalpel could cure people. But, unfortunately, I also had a brief love affair with a lifestyle I didn't have the means to support, even at the salary of a surgeon." Which turned out to be the reason Nancy had left him. Bye-bye, lifestyle… Bye-bye, Nancy. "But, ultimately, it got me in trouble."

"How?"

"I became greedy. Wanted more than I was entitled to."

"And you recognize that in yourself."

"What I recognized was that my boat got repossessed, and my car towed off because I couldn't afford it. What I also recognized was that the condo I'd bought was far too expensive for me, and the woman to whom I was engaged was far too rich to come down to my means."

"And so it ended?"

"Because she was rich, I wasn't, and I was trying to play a part that wasn't suited for me. Bottom line—I loved it for a while, until I discovered I really didn't love it at all. That it was just me trying to face up to the fact that my life was pretty shallow—except for my work."

"So, to compensate, you were trying to come up to her standards? Is that why you hate rich girls, because you couldn't?"

"Don't hate them. Just avoid them." But, to be fair, he was in a place in his life where he was avoiding *all* women. The one he'd had hadn't wanted him for who he was, and that had hurt. What had hurt just as much was how he'd been taken in by it, how he'd been so blind to it. Now, he just didn't trust himself enough to get involved with someone else.

"Or give them a hard time."

"By that, I assume you mean the hard time I give you." It was his natural instinct taking over.

He knew that, and he was fighting hard to control it as Juliette didn't deserve his leftover resentment.

"You do give me a hard time, Damien."

"But you bear up."

"I shouldn't have to, though. And that's the point. I'm a good doctor. I'm working here free of charge. People who know me will say I'm a good person. I'm a dutiful daughter. But you don't see any of this because one look at me, and one failed bed-making attempt, and *all* you see is the rich girlfriend you used to have, which equates to you as bad. And that's where it all ends for you."

"It's not you, Juliette."

"No, it's your former fiancée, and I get that. But what *you* need to get is that whatever went wrong between you and her has nothing to do with me."

She was right, of course. But that didn't change the fact that he still had his fears. Was it a fear born out of envy, though? Had he tried to emulate Nancy's wealth because he envied it? Because, if that was the case, it didn't sit well with him. Didn't say much about his character, either.

"I don't underestimate you as a person, or as a doctor," he said, giving in to the idea that he was completely wrong in all this. "And if you're intent on continuing on at the hospital—"

"Intent on continuing on?" Juliette exploded. "If I'm intent on continuing on? Who do you think I am, Damien? Someone who just flits in and out at will?"

"Well, it *is* an awfully big leap for you."

"Like it was for you? Don't you think I can measure up to you?"

"Of course you measure up to me. It's just that I thought that with the hard time I've given you—"

"And are still giving me," she interrupted.

"OK, and am still giving you. And, coming from the background you do—"

"You mean pampered and spoiled?" she interrupted again.

Open mouth, insert foot once again. He was nothing but a big blunder where Juliette was concerned, and it was beginning to worry him that he might actually drive her away. "No, that's not it. What I'm trying to say is that, in my experience, people have good intentions at the start, but they become disillusioned pretty easily. Do you know how many people have showed up at the hospital, responding to my ads, the way you did, this past year?"

She shook her head.

"Seven, Juliette. Seven. *And only one stayed.* And he stayed because, at the time, he had nowhere else to go. So why should I expect that you're going to stay, because you *do* have someplace else to go."

"Because I gave you my word, Damien." Her voice softened. "Because I'm not like the rest of them." She reached over and gave his arm a squeeze. "And one day you're going to trust that."

"What I trust, Juliette, is that I'm living in a godforsaken jungle village because it's the only place I *can* live right now. It's the only place where I can just be myself. And there's nothing else to offer here."

"You offered me a job, and that's all I wanted. It's enough, Damien." She smiled at him. "Don't make it any more complicated than that, OK?"

He didn't deserve her niceness, but he was grateful for it. More than that, he was grateful to have her there beside him. In a life that had let him down as often as he'd let himself down, he had no reason to believe that Juliette would.

* * *

"Stop!" Juliette twisted around in her seat and stared out the window. "Over there, on the side of the road. Did you see him?"

"See who?" Damien asked, as he slammed his foot onto the brake.

"I don't know. Maybe a child. Maybe a small adult. I couldn't tell. But he was huddling in the bushes."

"Where?"

"About fifteen or sixteen meters back."

Damien engaged the truck into reverse and started to back up. "Tell me when to stop."

"Right across from that tree." She pointed to a fabulously large shaving brush tree. "And I didn't get a really clear look, but I did see something—someone. I'm sure of it."

Damien stopped the truck in the middle of the road, and they both hopped out. "Over there," she whispered, pointing to a particular clump of bushes that was moving, despite the fact that there was no wind.

"Are you sure it wasn't an animal? Because we do have big cats, and crocodiles. And killer ants."

"It wasn't a killer ant," she huffed out.

"Fine, I'll go take a look. You stay here in case, well…" He shrugged.

"It was a person, Damien. I'm sure of it."

"A person who's not coming out to greet us."

"Maybe he's injured."

"Maybe he doesn't like outsiders." Damien approached the bush, looked down for a moment, then turned back and signaled Juliette over. "Or maybe he's scared to death."

Juliette looked down, and blinked twice. There, concealed in the bushes, was a little boy. Dark skin. Scraggly black hair. Huge brown eyes rolled up at them. Quivering lip. Probably aged six or seven. "He's…"

"Lost," Damien said gently. "Probably confused." He took a step toward the child, and the child hunched down into himself even more. *"Cómo te llamas?"* he asked. What's your name?

The boy didn't respond, so Damien tried again. *"Hablas español?"*

The child didn't respond to that either, so Damien took another try.

"Hablas inglés?"

When a third response didn't come, Damien looked at Juliette and shrugged. "He's not admitting to speaking either Spanish or English, and he's not telling us his name, so I'm at a loss what to try next. Any ideas?"

"No. But I do know we can't leave him here like this."

"So what are we supposed to do with him?"

"Take him back to Bombacopsis with us, and ask if anyone there knows him. Or if anyone knows of someone whose child went missing."

"Or comb a thousand square miles of jungle to see if he's from an isolated family living God only knows where. Or see if we can get someone out from the Child Services Agency who will, no doubt, relocate him, put him in a group home and let him get lost among all the other lost children there. Or—we could leave him here and let his family come find him which, I'm sure, they will."

"That's not safe, Damien, and you know that! We can't leave him alone."

Damien shut his eyes and shook his head. "I know. But there's no guaranteeing that we could even get him in the truck, much less get him all the way back to Bombacopsis. He's not used to outsiders, Juliette. In fact, he's probably never even seen an outsider before."

"But that doesn't mean he's automatically afraid of us."

"No, it doesn't. But the people here aren't that trusting. At least, not until we prove ourselves to them. And he, most likely, is being raised by a family that avoids us."

"He's not running away from us, though. Just look at him. He's staying here, and I think that probably means he wants help."

"You've got some mothering instincts going, don't you?"

"That's a bad thing?"

"No, it's not. But I'm afraid it's the thing that's going to convince me to take this boy back to Bombacopsis with us, then figure out what to do with him once we get there. So, can you direct some of that mothering at him and get him into the truck, because I've got a tonsillectomy to perform, and I need to get back to the hospital as fast as I can?"

Good Lord, what was he doing, picking up a child off the side of the road? The sad truth was, there were a lot of children, on the sides of a lot of different roads. That was simply a fact of life. The other fact of life was that this little boy, if not rescued, stood a good chance of being found by someone who would force him into child labor on one of the plantations. Damn, he hated this! Hated the harsh existence that so many people were forced into.

"I can try." Juliette took a couple of steps closer to the child, then held out her hand to him. "I don't know if you can understand me," she said gently, "but I want to help you."

The boy pulled away from her, but made no attempt to run.

"I know you're scared. I would be, too, lost out here, all alone in the jungle. But we want to take you someplace safe, someplace where there are people who can help us find your family." She continued to hold her hand out to him. "We really do want to help you."

"Said to the little boy who looks too afraid to accept help." Damien took another step closer to the child and held out *his* hand. *"Permítame ayudarle."* Let me help you.

Juliette stepped back, amazed by what happened next. The child took hold of Damien's hand and stood. No hesitation, no fear. It was as if the boy instinctively knew he could trust

Damien. "Looks like you two are forming a bond," she said.

"OK, now what?" he asked, standing alongside the road, hand in hand with the little boy.

"We take him with us, like we discussed."

"Like *you* discussed," Damien said, leading the boy over to the truck. "I didn't discuss it."

"Your gruff side isn't working on me right now, Damien. I can see right through you, and what I'm seeing is a big softy."

"What you're seeing is total confusion. I don't know what to do about the kid."

"What I'm seeing is a man who's stepping up to something even though he's not sure about it."

Well, that much was true. He *wasn't* sure about it. Had never thought about taking on the responsibility for a child, never even for the short term. Didn't want that obligation because he was always sure there was someone else who could do it better than him. Daniel could do it better. He saw that with Maddie. Juliette could do it better. He saw that with this little boy. So, as for him stepping up to anything—best-case scenario was someone in Bombacopsis would know the boy and, by evening, Damien would have him reunited with his family. Worst-case scenario—well, Damien didn't want to think about that one. Didn't want to think about how happy Juliette looked sitting in the truck next to the boy. Didn't want to think about how that mothering instinct in her had turned him on.

Nope. He didn't want to think about any of that. In fact, all he wanted was to get back to the hospital and get on with Pabla's tonsillectomy. "Do you think he's hungry?" he asked Juliette. "Because I have a candy bar in my medical bag."

She smiled at him. "Yep, a big, *big* softy."

CHAPTER SEVEN

"IN THE EXAM ROOM?" Juliette shook her head in amazement. "You're going to perform a tonsillectomy in the exam room?"

Damien looked over his shoulder into the waiting area, to check on the little boy they were calling Miguel for a lack of a real name, and shrugged. "I have an exam room, hospital ward, a storage shed out back and a one-room hut in which I live. Which one of those places do you think I should turn into an operating room?"

"OK, so I'm overreacting. I get it. But Damien, you need a real surgical suite if you intend on doing surgeries here. Even minor ones."

"How about I add that to my list of needs, not to be confused with my list of wants, not to be confused with my list of desires. Which you'll find in the filing cabinet, filed under *nonexistent*, since I don't even have the means to buy the paper to write that list on. The government doesn't fund me here, Juliette. The people who use my services do, when they can afford to. And when they can't they cook me food and wash my clothes and clean my hut. They're also the volunteers you see doing odd jobs around the hospital."

"But you do have some income, don't you?" She knew that El Hospital Bombacopsis operated on a shoestring, but she'd never known just how short that shoestring was.

"Some. And I have my own personal money, which is seriously on the decline since it's all about expenditures now, and no income."

He was using his own money to fund the hospital? She knew Damien had it in him to be noble, but she was only now coming to realize just how noble he was. "Have you ever thought about trying to find a benefactor? I know that can't happen in any of the villages because the people are usually too poor, but you could go into San José, or even back to the United States. I'm sure someone somewhere would be willing to donate to your hospital." She'd seen generosity at work all her life, seen what it could do. So why couldn't some of that generosity she'd come to count on go toward this ragtag little operation?

"And what would I have to offer them in return? A plaque over the door dedicating the building to them—a dedication that most of the people here won't be able to read? Or maybe I could name one of the beds after them? I mean, people who donate money do so for a reason, and we're fresh out of reasons here. There's no glory in it, no bragging rights, no visibility. So why bother?"

"That's a little jaded, isn't it?"

Damien shrugged. "It's all I've ever seen."

"So it gets back to your aversion of the wealthy." A very limiting aversion as she knew people out there who would donate simply out of their need to make a difference and their desire to see less fortunate people receive good medical care. Her father was one of those people. She'd watched him write checks for worthy causes all her life.

"Well, if you happen to run into one of them, tell them my door is open to them 24/7. But don't hold your breath, Juliette. This hospital's been operating hand to mouth for ten years, and none of them has ever shown up yet. And I'm not expecting that they ever will, even though your naive view of the world is telling you just the opposite."

"My view of the world is based on what I

know—based on generosity I have seen all my life." And sure, she hadn't traveled as much as Damien had, or seen as much as he'd seen, but she trusted that people were basically good—something Damien apparently didn't trust, and that made her feel sad for him. To have so much to offer, and to keep it buried away under such deep resentment—it was a waste. "And I know people, Damien. Generous people I can contact in due course."

"You know people who keep themselves locked into a tight little clique. And I'm not criticizing you for that, Juliette, because I don't think you've ever had the opportunity to spread your wings and see what's out there in this world."

"But you have?"

Damien nodded.

"And what you've seen—it's all ugly?" Had the man never witnessed true generosity and goodness? Or was he just too wounded to accept that it could exist?

"Not ugly. Just harsh. And not as giving as you seem to think it is."

"Maybe that's because you've never taken the time in the right places to find beauty and happiness, and optimism. But I know it's out there, Damien. I've seen the good in so many people. You just have to look for it. Expect it."

"Like I have to look for donors for the hospital, and expect that out of the goodness of their hearts they'll want to help us here?" He shook his head. "I've gone knocking on dozens of doors, asking for donations, only to have them slammed in my face. Asked pharmaceutical companies for donations and been denied. Approached medical equipment companies for anything they want to get rid of and, as you can see from what we have around here, failed miserably at that, too. I've turned up too many rocks, Juliette, and I know what's underneath them—nothing!"

"Yet you're here, doing good, in spite of all your rejections. Going into debt, taking a physical beating, getting lashed emotionally more than you'll ever admit, and you dare to tell me there's no good?" She shook her head and smiled at him. "Nope. You're wrong about this, Damien. I'm looking at good right now, and you give me the hope that there's so much more of it out there to be found. All you have to do is look for it. And that doesn't mean just turning up rocks to see what crawls beneath them. Although I'm sure if you turn up enough rocks you're bound to find something good there, too."

"What in the world did I do to deserve little Miss Optimism?" he groaned.

"You ran an ad, remember? And if you didn't want optimism you should have stated, *Optimists and believers and people who have a general sunny outlook needn't apply.*"

"That's exactly what the ad said when I applied," George said as he walked into the hospital. "Which is what got him *me*."

"And I'm glad to have you," Damien reminded him, smiling.

"Good thing, since I'm not leaving." George patted Damien on the shoulder as he walked by him and entered the exam. "Now, what about this tonsillectomy?"

This was an interesting dynamic, to say the very least, Juliette observed. Not just Damien and George, but the whole hospital and all its workings. And the more she was here, the more she was growing to like it.

"So while you two are operating, what do you want me to do?" she asked. "Oh, and, Damien.

I'm not giving up on you and the whole donation thing. You *need* an operating room, and there's going to be a way to get it." Even if she had to fund it herself, which was actually an appealing idea.

"You're not going to be here long enough for that to happen. In fact, I probably won't, either."

"We'll just see about that," she said cheerfully.

"Stop that!" Damien said.

"What?"

"Being so damned optimistic."

"You afraid it's contagious?" She took the stethoscope off his neck and put it around her own. Damien responded by heaving out a defeated sigh, but the twinkle shining in his eyes spoke of something other than defeat. Juliette wasn't quite sure what she was reading there, but she liked it, whatever it was. "Now, tell me what I need to do."

He bent down and whispered in her ear, "I'm not taking your money," he warned, then straightened back up.

She smiled up at him. "Who said I was offering it?"

"Your eyes."

"You read all that in my eyes?"

"I read all kinds of things in your eyes," he said with a seductive arch of his eyebrows. "And I meant what I said."

"So what if I march in here with a brigade of contractors ready to build you a proper OR?"

"How well do you withstand punishment?"

A slow smile crossed her face. "What kind of punishment are you offering?"

"Juliette, I mean it…" he said, squaring his shoulders, trying to put on a rigid face. And failing.

She laughed. "Just tell me where you want me to work. OK?"

He shook his head in surrender. "Do you always win?"

"I don't know. I've never really tried. But I'm liking the feel of this."

"And I'm not."

"Then we agree to disagree. Good!"

"You're incorrigible," he accused, finally giving in to his own smile.

"I'm working really hard at it, so I hope so. Now, about my assignment…"

"Fine. You win—*this round*. But only because

I need to get to work. So, for you—take care of Miguel for starters. Make sure he gets fed. Get him washed up, get his hair combed. Padre Benicio's going to come and take him to the festival so people there can see if they know him."

"And if no one does?"

"Then we give him a bed for the night, and approach the problem from a new perspective in the morning."

"If I'm attending to Miguel, who's going to look after the patients in the ward?"

Damien grinned. "You are."

It sure sounded as if it was all adding up to a busy night. Owing to the fact that she was already a little draggy, she wasn't sure how far her limited reserve of energy was going to take her. But she'd be darned if she'd let it show to Damien. For a reason she didn't understand, it was important that he saw her as capable in everything she attempted. His opinion of her mattered more than she wanted it to. "Then I guess I've got my work cut out for me, don't I?"

"Did I mention that you also need to supervise Diego? He's coming in tonight to do some filing for me since his mother is going to be out, delivering meals to some of the village's shut-ins."

"Two little boys, several sick people—anything else? Any beds that need changing? Or windows that need washing? Floors needing a good scrubbing?"

Damien chuckled. "Well, you might have a few inebriated partygoers wander in later on. This is the first night of Festival del Café, a celebration of the good fortune they receive from their coffee crops. Singing, dancing, food, beer—they really know how to put on a good party and usually we get some of the casualties of that *fun*. But don't worry, I should be done with my tonsillectomy before anything gets too out of hand."

Juliette shook her head. Well, so much for the little nap she'd hoped to sneak in sometime during her shift. "Fine, I'll get myself ready."

"You don't sound so enthused."

"I'm just...just worried about Miguel," she said. "That's all." That plus a definite lack of sleep these past few days.

"Well, just keep your fingers crossed that someone at the festival knows him."

An hour later she was still keeping her fingers

crossed, as Padre Benicio took hold of Miguel's hand and escorted him out of the hospital.

"Where's his *madre y padre*?" Diego asked. He was currently working in the G section of the file drawer, putting away folders and sorting the ones that were already in there.

"We don't know. That's why he's going out to the festival tonight. To see if anyone there knows who he is."

"Doesn't he know who he is?" Diego asked in all seriousness.

"He hasn't talked since we found him, so I have no idea if he knows who he is or not."

"Will he come here to work for el doctor Damien, the way I do?"

She wondered if Diego was fearful for his position here. He had such an affinity for Damien, much like the way Miguel did, that she suspected Diego was scared to death of being replaced. "I'm not sure what we're going to do yet, Diego. Right now, we're just hoping to find his parents." She was happy both boys responded so positively to Damien. And Damien was so kind to the boys, even though he tried to hide it. It was a side of him that made him sexy and likable and all kinds of other good things she didn't want to acknowledge.

"That would be good," the boy said. "Very good."

An hour after that, though, *very good* hadn't panned out, as Padre Benicio returned to the hospital with Miguel in hand. "No luck," he said to Juliette, who was in the middle of doing routine patient assessments.

Huddling over a patient who was being treated for general flu symptoms, she looked up at the priest and took her stethoscope earpieces out of her ears. "No one?" she asked him.

Padre Benicio, an older gent with a round belly, thinning brown hair and kind gray eyes, shook his head. "No one has heard about a missing child, either. And I talked to everybody in the streets."

"Well, I appreciate what you've done." What she didn't appreciate, though, was the outcome as her heart ached for the little boy. "So, what do you think we should do next? Does the church have some provision to take care of lost children?"

"In Bombacopsis, no. I could keep him in my cottage, if that would help you for a little while, but I think you're going to have to go to Child

Services in Cima de la Montaña to see what they suggest."

She already knew what they'd suggest. Damien had pointed that out so clearly. "Or we can keep him here at the hospital for a few days and hope that someone from outside Bombacopsis comes in and recognizes him." How Damien would feel about this, she didn't know. But she suspected he'd be agreeable, in spite of the protest he might put up. "Leave him here for now, and I'll talk to Damien once he's out of surgery. If he doesn't want to keep Miguel here, one of us will bring him to you later on tonight."

"Do you understand any of this?" Padre Benicio asked Miguel.

The boy looked up at him but didn't answer, and Juliette sighed a weary sigh. "He hasn't said a word since we found him."

"I'm sure he'll speak when he's ready, won't you, Miguel?" Padre Benicio said, as he let go of Miguel's hand and backed toward the hospital door. "In the meantime, I'll be at the festival if you need me."

If she needed him. Truthfully, she didn't know what she needed. Miguel's parents, a nap, a few extra hours in the day to accomplish everything she needed to…

"No luck," she said to Damien, once she noticed that he'd emerged from the exam room. "Looks like Miguel's ours to take care of for the time being."

"What it looks like to me is that you need to take a break. You look exhausted." He held out his hand to Miguel, who scampered across the corridor to take hold of it.

"It's nothing that a good cup of coffee won't fix."

"Well, if I thought that was true, I'd send you down to the festival to get one. They serve extraordinary blends at several of the roadside vendor stalls. But I think your tiredness goes beyond that."

"Are you diagnosing me?" she asked him, touched that he was noticing her so closely.

"Just worrying about you. You're running yourself into the ground, and I think you need to go over to my hut, where it's quiet, and take a nap."

"You know what they say…"

"That you'll sleep when you're dead?"

She nodded. "I'll be fine, Damien. But I appreciate your concern." This was a nice moment between them and she didn't want it to end, but Miguel needed to get settled down for the night, and she wanted to get onto the rest of her patients. So, reluctantly, she turned her back on Damien and returned to the ward, to the patient who was suffering complications from an infected puncture he'd got when, trying to grab its fruit, he fell out of a milk tree.

As Juliette lifted the bandage on her patient's right leg, she caught a glimpse of Damien standing in the doorway to the ward. He was staring at her. Holding on to Miguel and staring. It made her nervous, caused her to become self-conscious. So she tried her best to turn her back to him, but she knew he was still staring. She could feel it igniting a flame up and down her spine.

So what was *this* all about? She'd encountered all kinds of people before, in all kinds of places, but none of them had ever affected her like Damien. None of them had ever made her go weak in the knees or caused her pulse to quicken. None of them had ever distracted her so much. And she was distracted, make no mistake about that. In fact, she was so distracted she almost put the soiled bandage back on her patient's leg. Almost—but she caught herself before she did. Chastised herself for the absent-mindedness. Berated herself for the straying thoughts that were trying to grab hold of her.

The thing was, she wasn't even sure she liked Damien. That caused her the most concern. The man was affecting her in odd ways, ways she couldn't anticipate, and there were moments she couldn't even stand being in the same room with him. Of course, there were also moments when she wanted to be in the same room with him, in the same space, breathing the same breath. And those moments were seriously overtaking the other moments.

So maybe she did need that nap. Maybe it could cure her of whatever was ailing her. Only problem was, she wasn't sure there was a cure for *that—if that was, indeed what was happening.* Or if she even wanted to be cured if it was.

Pabla was sound asleep when Damien went to check on her. Doing nicely after her tonsillectomy. Juliette was in the bed next to the girl, sound asleep, as well. As much as he needed her help with the influx of partygoers from the festival trooping into the waiting room, he truly didn't want to disturb her. But George had gone home after the tonsillectomy, Alegria was off for the night and, with the exception of Miguel, who was bedded down in one of the ward beds, the patients already admitted and Diego, who was busy taking the names of potential new patients coming into the hospital, he was all by himself. And, from the looks of things, this was going to turn into one hell of a busy night.

"Juliette," he said quietly, still on the verge of not disturbing her.

"Do you need me?" she asked, looking up at him groggily for a moment, then bolting straight up in the bed. "I didn't, did I?" she asked, rubbing her eyes, then her forehead.

"What? Take a nap?" The expression on her face was frantic, almost like a deer caught in the headlights. For a moment, all he wanted to do was reach out, take her hand, pull her close and hold her. Reassure her. But, of course, he didn't. Urges like that had no place here. No place in his life, either. If he did allow them to take hold of him, though, it would have been with Juliette.

Right here. Right now. In his arms. Loving the feel of it. Savoring the emotional foreplay. Nice thoughts, but too distracting…

"I didn't mean to, Damien. I'm sorry." She pushed off the edge of the bed, stood and tugged her scrubs back into proper place. "I sat down, thinking I'd rest here next to Pabla for a minute, just to keep an eye on her, and I must have…" She looked over at the young girl who was sleeping peacefully in the next bed. "How long was I asleep?"

"About an hour."

"Why didn't you wake me up?"

"I assumed you needed the sleep. It happens, Juliette. We all get to that point where we just break down. I figured you'd reached that point." He reached over and squeezed her arm. "And you looked so peaceful I didn't have the heart to wake you up—until now, when I need your help."

She looked up at him. "Damien, I don't put in nearly as many hours as you do, and most of my work isn't that physically demanding. I shouldn't have been so exhausted."

He chuckled. "Why not? You're only human, like the rest of us."

"But I didn't come here to sleep. I'm still up to pulling off a few straight shifts without..." She frowned, and drew in a deep breath. "Maybe I'm getting too old to do this, and I'm just kidding myself thinking I still can."

"Juliette, are you feeling all right?" Something about her seemed a little off this evening, and he worried that her hours here at Bombacopsis were proving too much for her to handle. It was a different kind of medicine than she was used to, in a harsher environment than she'd ever dealt with. He'd had to make some physical adjustments when he'd first arrived or he'd have burned out too quickly. Better nutrition. Sleeping whenever he could. Asking for help when he needed it rather than plowing through by himself. Maybe that was all Juliette needed—some adjustments. He hoped so, anyway.

"I'm fine. Better now that I've wasted half the shift sleeping."

"Don't beat yourself up. I had a med student once who sat down on the side of the patient's bed to take an assessment, and fell asleep right there. When the nurse on the floor called me down to have a look at what she'd just found, I walked in on my med student all cozied up with his patient, snoring away like he didn't have a care in the world."

Juliette laughed. "What was the patient doing?"

"Looking stricken, and fighting not to get pushed out onto the floor."

"Well, if you ever catch me literally falling asleep on my patient, do me a favor and fire me on the spot so I don't have to go to the trouble of resigning."

Damien stepped closer to her and put his arm around her shoulders as they headed to the desk at the entry to the ward. They stopped for a second, Damien picked up the clipboard listing all the patients waiting to be seen and, with his arm still around her shoulders, they continued on toward the waiting room. "Are you good to take on a few patients? Because the festival is ending for the night and we've got them lining up for us now."

"What are the chief complaints?" she asked.

"Nothing serious, as far as I've seen. Mostly cuts, scrapes and bruises from too much merrymaking."

She stopped, then looked up at him, clear confusion written all over her face. “How?”

“Too much booze leads to shoving and hitting. Or people falling down or stumbling into things. Like I said, nothing serious. But what you get are a lot of the men who don’t want to go home in their condition, don’t want their wives or families to see what they’ve been up to, so they come here first. It’s sort of a village tradition, I’ve been told.”

“How long does this festival last?”

“Two nights.”

They started to walk again. “Well, sounds like a fun evening.”

“Diego’s giving them all numbers as they come in. How about you take the evens and I’ll take the odds? And we’ll both keep an eye out for serious problems that need to be seen immediately.”

“So you’ve got an eleven-year-old boy on triage?”

“Almost eleven.” Damien chuckled. “And I’m betting this isn’t exactly the way your father would run a hospital, is it?”

She laughed. “Damien, this isn’t the way *anybody* would run a hospital.” In spite of that, she was growing to love it here, every underfunded, understaffed minute of it.

"Miguel is not his name," George Perkins announced, stepping into the exam room. Juliette was busy on one side of it treating a patient for minor abrasions, while Damien was treating a head bump on the other side. "He's Marco. Marco de los Santos. He's seven. And he has a little sister, Ivelis, who's four."

Damien snapped his gloves off, tossed them in the trash and escorted his patient to the door; his patient reached into his pocket, grabbed out a few *colónes*, enough to total about twenty cents in US currency, and handed them to Damien in exchange for his medical care. *"Gracias,"* the man mumbled, then hurried on his way.

Damien turned to George. "So you've found the family?"

"Not exactly," George said. "I found someone at the festival who knew who Miguel—Marco—was. Told us where to find his family. Actually, his grandmother. In the jungle, in a pretty isolated little community. Marco and Ivelis have lived there with her since their mother died a couple years ago, according to the neighbor. Anyway, I took a couple guys from town out there and found…"

"His grandmother?"

George nodded, but the expression on his face told Damien there was more to the story. "So what's the bad news?"

"I think you found Marco on the road because he'd gone looking for someone to help his grandmother."

"She's sick?"

"She's dead, Damien," George said, practically whispering, so not to be heard. "Little Ivelis was sitting in a chair next to the bed, while her grandmother was laying there…"

"Dear God!" Juliette gasped. "That must have been horrible for the poor child."

"So what did you do with Ivelis?" Damien asked.

"Brought her back to Bombacopsis with me. Carmelita is looking after her now, but we really can't keep her since there's not enough room in our cottage, not with Carmelita and me, and her three children."

"And the grandmother?" Juliette asked.

"Padre Benicio is going to see to a proper burial. He's also going to make arrangements for the children."

"What kind of arrangements?" Damien asked.

"They've got no one. At least that's what the neighbor said. So the *padre's* going to talk to someone in Child Services in Cima de la Montaña this coming week and—"

"And they'll get lost," Damien snapped. "Separated from each other, and lost!"

"You can't be sure of that, can you, Damien?" Juliette asked, helping her patient down from the exam table and showing him to the door.

"No, I can't be sure of anything. But what I know is that there are so many abandoned children in Central and South America that all the protective agencies are too overrun to be effective. And what I know is that so many of the children who go into protective care don't fare well, especially older children like Miguel—Marco."

"But what else can you do?" she asked him. "Could Padre Benicio find them an adoptive family? Would Child Services allow that?"

"They'd love it. But it's an almost impossible task. Adopting out one older child is difficult, and to ask someone to take in two of them—there are too few resources to conduct that kind of a search for anybody who'd be willing to do that. And it would have to be done from here, because Child Services are so busy just keeping these kids alive from day to day, they don't have time to do much else."

"Which is why so many of these children are put into the fields to work," Juliette said, discouragement thick in her voice.

Damn, he hated this. Hated it to hell, as there was no real solution here for Marco and Ivelis. If only he'd just kept on going when Juliette had told him to stop, he wouldn't have known that these two children existed. Wouldn't have become involved in their lives. Ignorance would have been bliss for him in this whole situation. But not for Marco and Ivelis. And that's where his mind stopped and stayed—on the children. *Damn!* He *had* to find a way to help them.

"You'll figure it out, Damien," Juliette said, squeezing into the doorway next to him once George had left. "And you'll do the right thing by those children." She reached up and brushed his cheek. "I know you will." Then she scooted on by.

Damien watched her for a moment, the trace of her fingers still lingering on his cheek. How was it that someone he'd known for so short a time had made such an impression? But Juliette did make an impression, and it left him feeling—nice. Even happy.

"So tell me, Juliette, what's the right thing? Because I don't know," he said, following her through the ward, both on their way to do general assessments.

"I wish I could." She stopped, turned around to face him, then laid a reassuring hand on his arm. "I really wish I could."

He looked down at her, smiled wearily. Then kissed her. At first on the forehead. Then on the tip of her nose. Then full on her lips. A gentle kiss. A kiss of warmth and subdued passion. A kiss of need. It was a short kiss, though. Come and gone before he even realized what he'd done. But it left him feeling…stronger. And that was all he needed right now. Strength. Juliette's strength.

"I wish you could, too," he said, pulling her into his arms, and holding her tight to his chest.

CHAPTER EIGHT

THE WEEK HAD turned into a busy one for Juliette. She'd taken on twelve new placements, as well as spent time checking into various avenues of funding for Damien. Plus she'd met with a pharmaceutical representative who'd given her enough antibiotic samples to keep Damien's stock in decent supply for a few weeks. On top of that, she'd worried endlessly about Marco and Ivelis and what was going to happen to them. It was frustrating spending a whole week not knowing.

Given all the worrying, as well as all the other efforts expended on El Hospital Bombacopsis's behalf, she was coming to realize that she was getting too involved there. Too invested. But she couldn't help herself as the more she did, the more she wanted to do. To impress Damien, though? That thought had crossed her mind and she'd swept it aside as quickly as it had entered. Apart from Damien and any feelings she might be having for him, Juliette did like her short stay there every weekend. Liked the people. Especially liked the work.

Of course, there *was* that kiss. One simple kiss they hadn't talked about. One simple kiss that had caused her a week's worth of distraction. A kiss she could almost still feel on her lips.

"It's getting rough out there," she told Cynthia, as she packed an overnight bag to throw into her car for her weekend trip to Bombacopsis.

"The work, or your feelings for that gorgeous Dr. Damien?"

"Neither one. It's the involvement with the people. It's like I'm turning into a permanent part of the whole operation."

"Isn't that what you wanted?"

"I wanted some patient interaction, on a limited basis. I didn't want to get myself involved in day-to-day lives, and look at me. I've packed the whole backseat of the car with supplies I've managed to scrounge up for them." She sighed. "And I want to spend more time there than I have to give them."

"Is that a bad thing?"

"I don't know." Maybe she belonged back in

direct patient care on a full-time basis after all. Maybe both her father and Damien had been right about her all along. Two dominant men, both tugging at her life. She was trying to resist, but not sure she really wanted to anymore.

"Did you know that Damien is in town right now?" Cynthia asked her.

"He is?" That surprised her. Hurt her a little, too, as he hadn't thought to confide his plans to her. Not that he should have. But it would have been nice. Might have signaled something more than their brief kiss being only a whim. "Why?"

"He referred a patient to Carlos, and he came in to have a consult. I'm surprised no one told you about it."

"It's none of my business what goes on out there during the week." Brave words, to cover the fact that she was bothered.

"Yet when you leave here this afternoon, your car will be packed full of things that will be used to take care of matters you state are none of your business. And you spent hours on the phone this week, looking for contributions. How does that make sense, Juliette, if it isn't your business?"

"Damien does what he does, I do what I do. We

meet up on the weekends and work together, and that's as far as it goes." The problem was, he was taking up too much space in her thoughts now. Encroaching in places she'd never thought could be encroached upon. Putting notions into a head that had been previously blissfully notion-free.

"But you do have a working relationship, so shouldn't that count for something?"

"He didn't want to see me, Cynthia. Or else he would have let me know he was here." Truthful words, but they stung, nonetheless. She was getting in way too deep. Sinking down into the bottom of an undefined process that appeared to have no way out. Was she falling in love with him? In love for the very first time in her life?

"Look, I've got an appointment in twenty minutes. It should take me about an hour and after that I'll be back in the office for a couple hours. So if you're here when I get back we'll talk, and if you're not I'll see you when I get back Monday. Oh, and tell Carlos I said hello, and ask him if he could please do something to secure the towel rod in the kitchen."

"You should invite Damien to stay sometime. Maybe *he* could fix your towel rod."

"Except Damien and I aren't like that."

"You should be," Cynthia said, as she followed Juliette out the front door. "And you could be if you wanted to."

"You don't know that." Juliette turned to make sure the door was locked, then headed down the hall to the elevator in a casual stroll, Cynthia at her side. "Besides, Damien and I aren't really existing together under normal circumstances."

"Couldn't you make them normal?"

Could she? Honestly, Juliette wasn't sure what constituted normal with Damien. Wasn't sure he'd ever reveal that side of himself to her. Wasn't sure she'd recognize it if he did.

"Lunch?" Damien had promised himself he wasn't going to do this when he'd come to San José, and here he was, doing it, anyway. So what the hell was he thinking? Why was he trying to turn a perfectly good professional relationship into something else? "I was in the neighborhood, so I thought I'd stop by and ask."

Juliette spun around in her desk chair to face Damien. "I wasn't expecting you."

"I wasn't expecting me either, but here I am."

Approaching something he wasn't sure he should approach. "So, since it's lunchtime, I thought..." He shrugged.

Something about seeing her away from the hospital—she looked different. Not as confident as he normally saw her. Not as happy. And the stress he saw on her face—he'd never seen that in Bombacopsis, even when they'd performed a C-section bedside. "Are you OK?" he asked.

"Why wouldn't I be?"

"I don't know. Maybe because you look tired."

She smiled. "I'm fine. Just preoccupied."

"Do you want me to hang around and drive you to Bombacopsis later on?" He knew it was a feeble attempt to get some alone time with her, but it was the best he could come up with.

"If you did, you'd have to drive me back Monday morning, and that would put you on the road for half a day, coming here, going back to the hospital. So, as much as I appreciate the offer, I'll be fine driving out later on. Oh, and thanks for the lunch offer. It would have been nice, but I've got an awful lot to do between now and when I leave later today. But next time you come to San José—"

He was disappointed, but he wasn't surprised. Had he wanted a date with her, he should have asked properly rather than simply showing up and expecting it.

"Damien, why didn't you tell me you were coming?"

"Probably because we don't have to account to each other for anything. That's part of our relationship." A lame excuse, if ever there was one. He hadn't told her because he didn't know how to face her. And he didn't know how to face her because he wasn't sure about his emotions anymore. Or his dwindling resolve.

"What relationship, Damien? I work for you and, apparently, that's as far as we go."

"Is this about me kissing you?"

"It was just a kiss, Damien. Kisses happen all the time for no good reason."

"So you think I kissed you for no good reason?"

Juliette shrugged. "I don't know. But in my experience I don't take those things lightly. Maybe in your experience you do. But it's bothered me all week, because I've wondered if you have something more on your mind than only a professional relationship."

"Is that what you think we're doing? Forging a personal relationship?" In his mind, he believed that was exactly what they were doing. In a most awkward way. In a way that couldn't possibly work out for either of them as they were both headed in such different directions.

"Is it?" Juliette shook her head, and rubbed the little crease forming between her eyes. "Look, I have a lot of work to do before I leave for Bombacopsis, and I don't need to be distracted by this awkward dynamic we always seem to have between us."

"In other words, you're asking me to leave." Something he couldn't disagree with, considering the circumstances.

"Yes, I am."

"But you'll be in to work later on?" OK, so he knew he was on the verge of driving her away, but it was as if every time he got near Juliette he felt the need to retreat from her. Problem was, his way of retreating was all tied up in pushing her away. And he really didn't want to do that. But something always took him over, forced him into doing things he didn't want to do, saying things he didn't want to say. Was it simply that he expected Juliette to do the same thing to him that Nancy had done? Was he really *that* unsure of himself?

"I made a commitment to help you at the hospital, and I'll honor that, unless you say otherwise. So yes, I'll be there."

He was glad. Glad she could get around him. Glad she persevered in spite of his efforts to keep his distance. "I appreciate what you do, Juliette," he said, heading to the office door.

"Not enough, Damien. You don't appreciate it enough."

"You're right. I probably don't."

"And that's your problem, not mine."

It *was* his problem. Especially since thinking about Juliette had started keeping him up at night.

The three-hour drive seemed to take forever this evening, and when Juliette reached the edge of Bombacopsis she'd never in all her life been so happy to see anyplace as she was this one. First off, she intended to apologize to Damien for making it sound as if he had to account to her for his activities. He didn't. And she didn't want him thinking that she expected it. She also wanted to apologize to him for misinterpreting their relationship when, clearly, he had no intention of having anything other than a professional one with her.

Of course, that meant she'd have to quit reading more into it than was there. The kiss meant nothing. The personal interactions meant nothing. She was a colleague to him and she'd have to accept that, despite her growing feelings, or she'd have to leave. But she didn't want to leave.

This was where her inexperience in love was showing, and it embarrassed her.

Proceeding slowly down the main road, dodging potholes and barefoot children darting back and forth across the road, she looked to see if Marco and Ivelis were among any of them. But they weren't. She'd meant to ask Damien about them earlier, but her muddled thoughts had gotten in the way. So now she'd spent the better part of her three-hour drive imagining ways she would approach Damien and, alternately, worrying about the kids.

"Where are they?" she asked immediately upon entering the hospital. "Marco and Ivelis? Have you sent them to Child Services?"

Damien, who was busy rummaging through the file cabinet next to the single dilapidated desk in the exam room, turned to look at her. "They're with George and Carmelita right now. They've been looking after them during the day, when I'm working, and I've been looking after them at night, when George is working. It's not the best situation, but it beats having them locked up in an institution."

"Child Services are good with that arrangement?"

"Child Services are good with anything that doesn't add to their list. The kids are eating, they're being schooled at the church with the rest of the village's children, by Padre Benicio, and they have a roof over their heads—that puts them way ahead of the game, considering how things could be turning out for them."

"But it's only temporary, Damien. In the long term, what's going to happen to them?"

He shrugged. "Out here, you take it one day at a time. You know, get through the day and hope you make it to the next and, when you do, figure it out from there."

Would Damien actually take on the responsibility of tending to these children in the long term? Feed them, clothe them, continue them on at the school? *Love them?* In spite of his casual exterior, she saw a man who had great compassion, especially for children, so she was encouraged to believe that this could turn into a permanent situation. Damien as Dad. In an unexpected sort of way, it seemed to fit him.

"Look, Damien, I'm sorry for how I acted earlier. You're right. We don't have to account to each other for anything outside this job. But I was a little hurt. I mean, I'm not making a lot of friends in San José. Not enough time. And I suppose I thought we were becoming friends, then when you didn't tell me you'd be there, that just pointed out to me how wrong I was. I presumed too much."

"First, you didn't presume too much. We're friends, and I should have told you I'd be in town. That's what friends do, but I'm not very good at it. And second, I can't have a permanent relationship with you, Juliette," he said, quite directly. "Something other than friendship. If you thought I was leading in *that* direction, I'm sorry. I didn't intend that."

"Because I'm wealthy," she stated.

"No. It's because I'm not available. I came here to avoid those kinds of trappings, and I can't afford to get entangled again. I need space to sort my life. Space to figure out where I'm going and how I'm going to get there. Space to come to terms with what I've done in my past so I'm not doomed to repeat it in my future. Nancy, my biases, my envies—all the things that, for a time, turned me into someone I didn't want to be."

"And I take up your space?"

"In ways you probably wouldn't even understand."

"So that's it? We can be friends and colleagues. But that's all?" She wasn't surprised by the direction this conversation was going, but she didn't like it. Didn't like knowing that these strange, new feelings she was having were letting her down.

"Honestly, I don't know." He sighed heavily. "I didn't want you to make a difference in my life, other than in a professional way. But you're doing that, and I don't know what to do about it because it wasn't in my plan. I mean, I felt guilty as hell about not letting you know I'd be in San José, and I intended to do that because I was trying to distance myself from whatever it is we're doing."

"Because?"

"Because I'm trying *not* to fall in love with you."

Could that mean he *was* falling in love with her?

"Falling in love with me would be bad?" If this was the way love started, it was a lot more difficult than she'd ever imagined it to be.

"It's very bad because I don't want to get hung up on someone. I don't want to feel guilty when I decide to avoid a situation or don't meet personal expectations. I don't want to be distracted from the things I'm trying to accomplish both professionally and personally."

"I distract you?" This was leading to something depressing. She could feel it coming. And it scared her because the side of Damien she was seeing right now, the brutally honest side, was the one she desperately wanted in her life. But it frightened her because his truths were turning out to be painful.

"When I let you."

"Which leaves us what? Anything? Or do you

intend on running another ad to replace me?" In and out, just like that. It was almost too much to comprehend. "What do you think?"

"What I think, Juliette, is that I'm better off alone. It suits me. Keeps me out of trouble. Keeps me from putting myself in the position that I might not do the best work I can do."

"Then that's the answer, isn't it? I'll go, and you can find somebody else to replace me. Someone who won't mess with your mind the way I, apparently, am." Better to do this now, before she got in any deeper. But she certainly hadn't counted on how much it would hurt. And it did hurt. And now she was feeling light-headed and dizzy. Nauseated. Headachy. "Well, if it's OK with you, I'll stay on until my replacement arrives." Stay on to endure more of an emotional beating. Because she did have her obligations here, and she wasn't going to let him defeat that in her. Not while she had a shred of pride still intact. "So go ahead and assign me my work for the evening, and I won't bother you."

"Juliette, I—"

She held out her hand to stop him. "Look, Damien. All I want is to do my job, and skip the rest of this. OK? Just let me work." Which was all she should have ever done in the first place. But, stupid her, she'd stepped in too far.

"Fine. I have two patients down in the village I need to see, and I want to drop an inhaler refill off to Padre Benicio. Alegria is here, tending to some basic chores, and what I need you to do this evening is to admit Senõra Calderón when she shows up in a little while. She was complaining of symptoms that lead me to believe she might be diabetic, but when I tried to admit her earlier she insisted on going home and bathing first. So she should be back here anytime. Do an A1C—I have the test kit in the medicine cabinet. Also a general assessment for any signs of neuropathy, and take a comprehensive medical history. I mean, you know all this already, so I really don't need to tell you what has to be done. By the time you're finished, I should be back, and I'd like for the two of us to inventory our supplies—"

Business as usual, she thought. That was all she was to him—business as usual.

"—and then, after that, I want to check our medicines. Which should pretty well take us on into the night."

Couldn't he simply ask her not to go? Couldn't he say something to encourage her? Something? *Anything?* This was awkward. She felt it. He felt it. But there was nothing they could do about it. She was developing feelings for him, and she had no idea what he was developing for her, he was so back and forth about it.

"Anyway, I'll be back in a while." That was all he said. Then he walked out the door, and Juliette walked into the exam room, feeling numb.

Damn, he was stupid. She'd done all but admit to him that she loved him, and here he'd gone and thrown it right back in her face. How stupid could any one man get?

"Have you ever done something you knew you didn't want to do, but you did it, anyway?" he asked Padre Benicio.

The *padre* chuckled. "Too often, I'm afraid."

"I've got something good happening to me, and I know it's good, and I know I want it, but I'm doing everything I can to stop it because I don't know what kind of future I have. Whether it's here or someplace else. Whether it's as a jungle GP or a big-city surgeon. And if I don't know these things about me, how can I offer anything to anybody else?"

"Whose best interest do you have at heart in this?"

"Everybody's—nobody's. I don't know."

"Then maybe you should reevaluate this good thing that's happening to you and try to figure out if you want it badly enough to sort the rest of your life. Ask yourself what you're really afraid of. Because the jungle is a good place to hide, Damien. It has a way of sorting things for you, if you're not careful."

The *padre* was right, of course, as Damien wasn't sure he even knew how to go about *starting* to put his life in order, let alone proceeding through and finishing it. He was scared of changing his life, scared of changing himself, scared of coming to terms with what he *really* wanted. Which was Juliette. And now she was leaving. He'd pushed her too far. Pushed her in a direction he didn't want her taking. And he was the only one who could rectify that.

"Look, I've got to go try to straighten something out before it's too late." He prayed that he wasn't.

* * *

Hearing the approaching footsteps, Juliette looked up to greet her patient and was surprised to see Damien standing in the exam room doorway. "You just left," she said, trying to sound even when everything inside her was fluttering and flustering.

"I came back because I shouldn't have walked out and left things hanging between us, the way they are."

"You said what you wanted to say, Damien. What else is there?"

"That I don't want you to leave. That I look forward to Friday evenings, knowing that you're on your way here. That I don't know what to do with our friendship and I want you to try to help me figure it out."

This wasn't what she'd expected from him. Not at all. And she wasn't sure what to make of it. Wasn't sure of the way he swung back and forth.

"You know, I've never had a relationship other than friendship before."

"Never?"

She shook her head. "I've had casual dates, nothing serious, and no, I'm not a virgin. But anything that went beyond casual—" She shrugged. Life just hadn't permitted anything else for her, between her work commitments and the fear of what losing her might do to her father. Yes, dutiful doctor, dutiful daughter—all of it had caused her to miss out and now, here she was, practically clueless. "I don't know how to help you figure it out, Damien. If you want something more, you've got to figure out how to do it. And if you decide you really don't want anything other than what we've already got, that's fine. I'll accept it." Even though it would break her heart. "But the one thing you have to know is that if we go any further, I don't expect to be hurt."

"I wouldn't hurt you intentionally."

"But there are so many unintentional things you do. And sure, you have regrets and apologize, like you're doing now. But some things can't be undone. When you say the words, they can't be unsaid. Apologies may be accepted, Damien, but words still linger." OK, so she was putting it all on the line now, but what was there to lose except a little self-esteem?

"I didn't come here to fall in love, Juliette. I came to escape it. Had one serious experience with it, and it didn't work. And it scares me to think that I could go and do it again."

"I didn't come here to fall in love, either. I came to escape my father's dominance. I don't want to be dominated, don't want to be around anyone who believes he or she has that right."

"So where does that leave us?" he asked.

"It leaves us as two runaways with strong ideas of what we don't want, trying to define what we do want." And that pretty well summed it up. "We don't have to date, Damien. We don't have to get physical. We don't have to admit our feelings toward one another. But what we do have to do is realize that our friendship isn't just casual, nor is it just professional. If you can live with that—if *I* can live with that—then I can stay here. But if we can't live with what's apparently going to go unspoken, then I'll have to leave." It surprised her that she'd summoned the courage to say these things to him, but they needed to be said. And so far Damien hadn't made any effort to say them himself.

But she felt good about clearing the air. It gave her hope that even if she couldn't move forward with Damien, someday she might be able to move forward with someone else. Although she didn't think she'd ever find anyone who could compare to him. It was a thought that made her feel as if she'd just said her last goodbye to her best friend.

"I don't know what to say, Juliette. I mean, I appreciate your honesty. And I appreciate you."

He looked as if he were at a loss for something to latch on to. An explanation, a hope. It was something she'd never seen in him before.

"I don't want you to leave. I just don't… I just don't know how to handle you being here. So for right now, how about we let this blow over and see what happens in the future. OK? You know, get past it, and see what we've got left."

"So what do you want from me, other than work? Or do you even want anything?"

"Damned if I know," he said, slamming his fist into the file cabinet so hard the sound resonated out the door and down the hall. "I had this plan. I was going to come here for a couple of years, get away from all the trappings that almost ruined me before, try to find my worth again. All of it just me, by myself. I mean, who the hell ever goes to the jungle to hide and comes across someone like you?"

She laughed. "It goes both ways, Damien. I didn't expect to come to the jungle to find *you*."

"But here we are. And this *thing* between us is driving me crazy because I don't even know what it is."

He *did* know what it was. She was sure of it. But he was dancing all around it, coming so close, then backing away. And it was frustrating that he wouldn't, or couldn't, admit it. Not to her, not even to himself. As much as Damien had tried pushing her away, he was pushing himself away even harder.

"Then, by all means, distance yourself, Damien. Think as much as you want, and I'll stay out of your way so you'll have even more time to think." She didn't want to be cross with him, but his hot-and-cold switch was confusing her so much she didn't know how else to react. This *thing*, as he called it, was getting complicated—for both of them.

"You want me to take them back to the hospital and get them something to eat?" Damien asked George. "I hate dumping all this responsibility on you and Carmelita." The more he was around the children, the more he wanted to be around them. It was yet another new facet to his ever-baffling life.

George looked over at the two, who were playing in the churchyard, keeping a distance between themselves and the other children who were there for school. "We're good for dinner. How about we let them stay for that and I'll bring them back to the hospital in a couple of hours?"

Damien sighed. "I might be back by then, if I don't feel the sudden urge to get out of there and take another walk." Although walking, as he was doing now, wasn't a solution to what was bothering him. And what was bothering him was—him! He was disgusted with himself. Didn't know where all this uncertainty came from, as it was something new to him. Normally when he was interested in a woman he'd ask her out. They'd dine, dance, maybe make love at the end of the evening. Then he'd call her again, or he wouldn't. Whatever struck his fancy at the time. Of course, there was Nancy, and he'd thought she was the keeper.

But, in recent days, he'd even wondered about that. Wondered if his real motivation in that relationship was to prove to himself that he was worthy of climbing into higher circles, worthy of being embraced by the likes of Nancy's ilk more so than by Nancy, herself. Which made him pathetically lacking in character, and full of self-doubt. And it wasn't a stranger to him. He'd felt it recently when he'd gone to Daniel's wedding and saw what a wonderful life his brother had made for himself in the wake of a tragedy that many men would never overcome. He'd seen happiness and contentment and joy—things he'd never seen in himself. Things he'd never thought he could have, given his lifestyle choices. Things that made him desirous of something he didn't know how to get.

Home, family, all the trimmings—in other words, maturity. It was bound to happen at some point in his life, but he wasn't prepared for it the way it hit him. He'd actually looked forward to scaling back on his lifestyle, not running around so much, driving a family SUV rather than a sports car, maybe even mowing the yard on Saturday mornings. Yep, that was him. Craving the domestic after living the high life. But he'd picked the wrong person, and had actually convinced himself for a while that Nancy would do well living that life. Apparently, he'd been seeing things in her that just weren't there, though. Deluding himself. Which was why he'd come to the jungle. After Nancy, he'd needed to get away—from what he'd been, from what he'd hoped to become. Just get away from it all. Isolate himself from everything and try to figure out what was real in his world, because for so long nothing in his past had been.

"Are you and Juliette disagreeing again?" George asked, his eyes twinkling.

"Juliette and I aren't anything!"

"Maybe that's the problem," George said as he signaled Marco and Ivelis over to him. "Maybe you and Juliette should be doing something. Talking at the very least. Taking a walk together. Holding hands. Gazing into each other's eyes. You get the point anyway. I'll bring the kids back down to you later. Good luck with Juliette, by the way."

Talking? Walking, holding hands, gazing? Yes, good luck, but to whom?

Juliette looked at the results of the A1C test she had given Senõra Calderón and cringed. She was reading way above the normal for diabetes, which was a pretty good indication that the woman was afflicted. Damien had called it right and she wanted to consult with him to see what could be done to treat the woman, given that resources for diabetic treatment out here in the jungle were very limited. But he'd been gone for over an hour now, and she was beginning to wonder if he was coming back.

"I'd like to admit you to the hospital tonight, and have el doctor Damien talk to you when he returns."

"You can't talk to me? Because I like seeing a lady doctor."

That was flattering, especially in a village where old-school values prevailed and outsiders were viewed as intruders. Most notably, female outsiders. "El doctor Damien is going to be your doctor, not me, since I'm only here two days week. Which is why I want you to see *him*."

"Then I'll come back tomorrow when he's here. Right now he's at the Bombacopsis Taberna drinking *cerveza*, and he didn't look like he was going anywhere for a while." Senõra Calderón hopped off the exam table and went on her way, walking right by George, as he brought Marco and Ivelis into the hospital.

"Are you OK?" George asked Juliette on his way in the door.

"Just tired. Nothing big. What's the Bombacopsis Taberna?"

"The Bombacopsis Tavern."

"And *cerveza* is...?"

"Beer." He smiled sympathetically. "But he limits himself to one, just in case you were wondering. Oh, and Damien knows the kids are here."

"You talked to him?"

"Briefly, on my way here. He should be back anytime."

She wasn't going to hold her breath on that one. "So what am I supposed to do with them in the meantime?"

"Find them a bed and let them go to sleep. That seems to be the usual routine."

"That's a heck of a way for a child to live, isn't it?" Even though this arrangement was better than what they might have ended up with, she wanted better for them. Wanted them in a happy home. Normal life. Normal family.

"Damien means well, and I know he's trying

to do right by them. And he *has* been building a partition in his hut so the kids can have their own room there. It's just that these things don't get done too quickly when your resources are limited."

Was Damien actually setting himself up in a family situation? She liked the idea of that. Liked it a lot. The light on him, bit by bit, was shining much brighter. And it notched up even more thirty minutes later, when he entered the hospital ward and went straight to the beds she'd sectioned off for the children. He stood there looking at them, while she stood there looking at him. The tender expression for them on his face—it made her heart melt. Made her heart swell at the same time. For this was the real Damien. The one who kept himself hidden under so many layers of uncertainty. The one he probably didn't even know existed. The one she'd gone and fallen in love with. And yes, it was love, in spite of all its obstacles.

CHAPTER NINE

RUBBING HIS EYES and shaking himself, trying to stay awake, Damien took one last look into the waiting room and finally, after sixteen hours of back-to-back patients, it was empty, except for Juliette, who'd taken a moment to sit down and rest. She'd apparently fallen asleep. But who could blame her? She needed it, and that was really all he wanted for himself, as well. Several hours of uninterrupted sleep.

To sleep, perchance to dream... Dreaming that impossible dream... Dreaming dreams no mortal ever dared...

Damn, he was getting punch-drunk now. He shook himself again. Harder this time, trying to throw it off. But random thoughts were running rampant through his brain, which meant he was no good for anything. Especially not for anything as far as the hospital was concerned. So as soon as George came in to take over the shift, he was going to go back in his own hut. Take the rest of the afternoon for himself—no children, no patients. Nothing but perfect peace and quiet. And sleep.

But first he had to tend to Marco and Ivelis. He'd walked them down to the church for morning school earlier, and now it was time to take them back to the hospital for lunch. When he arrived, Padre Benicio was standing in the doorway, waiting for him, holding the children's hands. Just seeing them there—it caused a lump in Damien's throat. He wanted so badly to have more time with them. Desperately wanted to take Marco out to play ball, and Ivelis to one of the local women who cut hair. Wanted to read to them. Sit down to a quiet meal with them and ask them about their day. Wanted to…be a father? *Did he really want to be a father?*

No. He couldn't—*could he?* He thought about that for a moment. Thought about all the changes he'd have to make to accommodate children in his life. About how much he enjoyed having them around—and what might happen to them if he didn't allow them to stay. That was the thought that sobered him. Made him sick to his stomach because he knew what was waiting for orphans like Marco and Ivelis, and it was bleak. How could he let those children step into the kind of life that awaited them outside Bombacopsis? Which meant—well, it meant a lot of things. Changes in his life. Changes in his outlook. Changes in ways he couldn't even anticipate.

Could he do it? Could he take on two children when he refused to take on a real relationship with Juliette? How did any of that make sense?

"Any new developments with the children?" he asked Padre Benicio.

"Nothing's changed. They don't talk, don't go outside to play when the other children do. They don't do anything. So I was wondering, do you think it's time to take them somewhere and have them examined? See if there's something psychological that can be treated? I know I'm not a doctor, but I am concerned that they might have a condition of some sort."

Damien shook his head. "The only condition they have is an overwhelming sadness for the loss of the only security they had in this world. I imagine they're scared to death and they're drowning in everything that's going on around them."

"They need a family, Damien. Two parents together, or a mother or father, separately. Someone to look after them properly, and not do what we're doing here—trotting them from place to place, person to person. Dropping them into situations they couldn't possibly understand."

"I know that and, believe me, I'm looking at ways to take care of them." One way, actually, and he wasn't yet sure about it. Wasn't sure about anything.

"Damien, Child Services isn't going to list them as a priority now, since they already have a roof over their heads, they're being fed, bathed and schooled. As far as the child authorities are concerned, these children are in a good situation. They're not going to change that, since they've got so many other children to deal with who are in horrible situations."

"I know," he said. "Their prospects aren't good."

"Unless they stay here, with you."

He shook his head. "I've been thinking about it. But sometimes I'm barely able to make it on my own as an adult, and I certainly shouldn't be dragging two children along into that. They're great kids, but they deserve better than me." That much was true. They did.

"They deserve to be happy, Damien, however that happens. And whoever that happens with. And I don't think what you consider to be a lack of stability would matter at all as long as you love them."

"Look, Padre. I'm doing the best I can, with what I have. It's not good enough, but it's all I can do. And I'm well aware of my limitations." The biggest one being how turning himself into a single dad scared him to death. As much as he cared for those kids, he didn't know if he could do justice by them.

"We all have limitations, Damien. But the real measure of a person comes not in what he knows he can do, but in what he doesn't know he can do and still does in spite of himself. Think about that for a while. And, in the meantime, I'm going to go find a nice *casado* for lunch, then I'll come down to the hospital to get the kids and take them back to the church for afternoon school." He tipped his imaginary hat to Damien, and scooted out the door, leaving Damien standing there, with Marco on his left side and Ivelis on his right.

"Well, let's go see what Rosalita has fixed for your lunch." He extended a hand to each child, and the three of them wandered off toward the hospital, looking like a perfect little family.

"Juliette?" Damien gave her a little nudge. She was still asleep. Three hours now. And she was sitting up in one of the chairs in the waiting room, looking totally uncomfortable. He should have insisted she go to bed hours ago, but he hadn't had the heart to wake her. Now he wished he'd found that bed for her, as he could practically feel the stiff muscles she'd have when she did wake up. Which would be in about a minute since he wanted to make sure she got something to eat before Rosalita got busy with dinner preparations.

"Wake up, Juliette. We need to get some food in you." And he needed her company, if only for a few minutes. Missed it when he didn't have it.

"Not hungry," she mumbled, turning away from him without opening her eyes. "Let me sleep another few minutes."

"After you've eaten." He nudged her gently

again, then frowned. Stepped back. Took a good hard look at her. And his face blanched. "Juliette, do you understand what I'm saying to you?"

"Yes," she said, dropping her head to the left side, resting it on her shoulder. "And I'll get back to work in a minute."

"Juliette, listen to me. I want you to look at me. *Open up your eyes and look at me.*"

"They're brown, Damien. Dark brown. Nothing extraordinary." She opened her eyes wide for him to take a look. "See?"

Damien uttered an expletive and immediately reached down to feel her forehead. Then uttered another expletive. She was burning up! Fever, fatigue… "Do you have a headache?" he asked, grabbing his stethoscope out of his pocket and positioning it in his ears.

"Only because I haven't had enough sleep lately," she said, finally starting to rouse, starting to stand. But Damien pushed her gently back into her chair.

"Stay there while I listen," he instructed, sticking the bell of the stethoscope just slightly into the top of her scrub shirt.

"What?" she asked, her face beginning to register slight alarm. "What are you looking for?"

He held his finger up to his lips to shush her. Then listened, first to her lungs, then her heart, then her lungs from the back. "Any joint pains?" he asked when he'd finished his cursory exam. "Or vomiting?"

Now she looked totally alarmed. "What aren't you telling me?"

"Any joint pains or vomiting," he repeated, trying to sound as calm as he possibly could, when nothing inside him felt calm.

"No, and no. Now, tell me!"

"Before you came to Costa Rica, what were you vaccinated for?"

"Typhoid, Hep A and B, malaria…"

"And you're up-to-date?" He looked down at her. "With everything?"

"What's wrong with me, Damien?"

"I need blood tests to confirm…"

She bolted up out of her chair, but was struck by a sudden, severe dizziness, and almost toppled over. Toppled into Damien's arms instead and, rather than pushing away from him, stayed there as he wrapped his arms around her close. "Is it malaria?" she asked, her voice now trembling.

"Your eyes are jaundiced, Juliette. And the rest of your symptoms…" Damn, he hated this. Her onset was too fast. Her symptoms growing too severe far too soon before they should have. Nothing about this was as gradual as he'd seen before, and that worried him. Malaria was bad enough, but with this kind of reaction to it— "And you're showing all the usual symptoms." Of all the diseases he'd treated here, he hated malaria the most.

"I can't have malaria, Damien. I was vaccinated!"

Worldwide, malaria killed nearly half a million people every year and infected over two-hundred million.

Soon after he'd arrived in Bombacopsis, a small outbreak of it had taken eleven villagers. It had swooped in and killed them before he'd even known what was happening. But he didn't want Juliette to know that. Didn't want her to know that, right now, he was scared to death for her. "I'm afraid you do have it, sweetheart," he whispered gently, stroking her hair. Wiping the fever sweat on her face onto his shirtsleeve.

"Damien..." She nestled tighter into him.

"Shh," he said tenderly. "I'm going to take care of you."

"But if the vaccine didn't work..."

Then there was a good chance the limited antimalarial drugs he had on hand might not work, either. It was unthinkable. But he had to face it.

Damn, he wanted to take her to San José, put her in a proper hospital, hold her hand while she got cured there, but he was sure she couldn't make it that far. Especially now that she was starting to tremble in his arms. Hard trembling. Paroxysms. Soon to be a spiking fever, plummeting in the blink of an eye to a below-sustainable life temperature, then spiking back up and plummeting back down again. Over and over until coma. Then death—

No! That wasn't going to happen. He wouldn't let it. "It will work," he said, hating himself for giving her an empty promise. "I'll take care of you, Juliette. Whatever you need, whatever I have to do, I'll take care of you."

"Promise?" she whispered.

"Promise," he whispered back. But she didn't

hear him as she'd slumped even harder against him, exhaling a long sigh.

Juliette remembered being swept up into Damien's arms, then being carried across the hall and placed gently down on the exam table. Remembered the tender way he'd examined her, started her IV, sponged her down with cool water, removed her fever-drenched clothing and put her into a hospital gown. She even remembered him carrying her out to a bed in the ward, and pulling the protective screens around her for privacy. After that, though, she remembered nothing. It was all a blank. A vague cloud in her mind that concealed something she couldn't find.

"How long have I been out?" she asked, as Damien appeared at her bedside, preparing to change her bedding.

"You're awake!" he said, his voice sounding almost excited.

"I think I am. Not sure, though." She reached up to brush the hair back from her face and saw the IV running in her right arm. Saw the old-fashioned green oxygen tank sitting next to her bed. Saw the darkness coming from the window above her head. "Is this still Sunday?" Sunday night. Late. Yes, it had to still be Sunday, as she remembered working earlier.

"It's Thursday," Damien said, setting the bed linens down on a chair. "Thursday night, almost midnight."

"No," she protested, shaking her head. "It's Sunday. I'm just tired from overworking."

"You're tired because you have malaria, sweetheart. And the last time you worked was four, almost five days ago."

Nowhere in her mind was she prepared to process this. Nowhere in her mind was she prepared to accept it. "Damien, I don't see how..." She shook her head. "You've got to be wrong. I haven't been sleeping for four days!"

"No, you weren't sleeping. Not exactly, anyway."

"I was unconscious? In a coma?"

Damien nodded, then sat down on the edge of her bed, and took hold of her hand. "You have malaria. An advanced case of it. And you collapsed Sunday night."

"But I remember Sunday night, and I wasn't feeling that bad." Medically, she understood this.

Understood the gravity of it. But emotionally—she couldn't grasp it. She hadn't felt sick. Just tired. Down-to-the-bone tired. Nothing some proper rest wouldn't have cured. Malaria, though? "I don't recall that I had any symptoms."

"You didn't. Not up until just a few minutes before you collapsed."

"And you've been treating me with?"

"Quinine and doxycycline."

The same combination they would have used in any hospital in San José. But they'd had such a limited supply on hand. How had he sustained her for so long on what they had? "How?" she asked.

"I have my ways," he said, offering no further explanation, dipping his hand into his pocket to finger the exorbitant bill that came with an overnight express delivery out in the middle of a jungle. A bill he'd paid himself as the hospital had no funds for it.

But she wanted to know what they were. Not that it made a difference to her one way or another, but that was what her mind was fixed on now. She was fighting to make sense of things she couldn't... But the drugs—they made sense to her. She understood them, even though she understood little else. “Where did you get them, Damien?” she persisted.

“Why is it so important to you?” he asked.

“I don’t know. I’m…confused. I can’t think. Can’t focus. But the drugs you used—I remember them, and I remember you didn’t have enough of them. I wanted to bring you some. I remember that. I put it on my list of things I wanted to find for the hospital.”

“You have a list?” he asked.

“Things you need.” Things that she couldn’t remember yet. But she did remember there was such a need here. A need she’d wanted to fix for some reason that had also vacated her memory.

“You never told me.”

“I didn’t?”

Damien shook his head.

“I should have. Don’t know why I didn’t.” Was she involved here in something more than merely being a doctor? Juliette studied Damien’s face for a moment. Was she involved with *him*?

“It’ll come back to you, Juliette. In time. Your brain is suffering a trauma right now, with the malaria, but you’re getting better.”

“I hope so,” she said, as her eyelids began to

droop. “I really…” She didn’t finish her sentence. Couldn’t finish it, as she dropped back off to sleep.

So Damien waited until he was sure she wouldn’t wake up, then changed the bedsheets underneath her, and kissed her on the forehead. “You’ve still got a way to go, Juliette,” he whispered, as he pulled a sheet up over her frail body. “But you’re going to make it. I promise, you’re going to make it.” Wishful thinking? Empty promise? He didn’t know, as she was clearly not out of the woods yet. But hearing the words, even though he’d been the one to speak them, made him feel better.

Damien searched for twenty minutes before he found Marco and Ivelis. Twenty long, panicked minutes. Padre Benicio had brought them home from school, left them outside the hospital to play, and when Damien had gone to call them inside they were nowhere to be found. Frantically, he’d searched the property, looked in the supply shed, run to the church to see if they were there. But no one he’d asked knew where they were, no one had even seen them, leaving Damien to wonder if they were trying to get back to their home. Trying to get back to that one place where they felt secure.

He'd been so preoccupied with Juliette these past few days—caring for her, holding her hand, talking to her even though she was unconscious again. He hadn't meant to neglect the children, but he had, and he felt guilty as hell. Now, he was nearing nausea, he was so worried, as he headed back to the hospital. To think Padre Benicio had actually suggested to Damien that he keep the children! How could he, when he couldn't even keep an eye on them for a few minutes?

"No luck," he told George, as he entered through the hospital's front door. "I'm wondering if they're trying to go home."

George gave him a sympathetic smile. "There's something you need to see," he said, pointing into the ward. "Or two young people you need to see, rather."

"But I searched the ward first," Damien said, clearly perplexed.

"Not all the ward, you didn't."

"Then they've been here all along?" His heart felt suddenly lighter.

"Like I said, there's something you need to see."

He gestured for Damien to follow him, and he stopped at the end of Juliette's bed, on the other side of the partition. "Take a look."

Damien pushed one of the partitions aside and there, standing next to Juliette's bed, were Marco and Ivelis. Just standing there, looking down at Juliette. Not moving. No facial expressions. Nothing. It was a curious sight. But a nice one. Juliette surrounded by children. It suited her, and he only wished she'd wake up again so she could see what he was seeing. "Thank you," he whispered to George, as George backed away then returned to the clinic.

Damien stepped closer to Juliette's bed, and stopped next to Marco. But he didn't say a word. Instead he just put his arm around the boy, and held out his other hand to Ivelis, who clasped on immediately. And they simply stood there together. For how long? Damien didn't know. A minute? An hour? An eternity? It really didn't matter, as he was so relieved that everything else around him faded into a blur and all his concentration was on this, right here, right now.

"Por qué la señora duerme tanto?" a tiny voice finally asked. Why does the lady sleep so much?

It was Marco asking. A voice of concern where previously there had been no voice.

A lump formed in Damien's throat, causing his own voice to go thick. *"Porque ella está muy enferma."* Because she's very sick, he answered, trying hard not to show how affected he was by one simple sentence. But he was affected, and it was strange that he would be, as he was trying hard not to care for these children. To be custodial, yes. But to care—

"Cuando ella va a despertar?" When will she wake up?

Damien bit down on his lip.

"No sé. Realmente, no sé." I don't know. I really don't know. Words he almost choked on.

Marco accepted this, and nodded. Then he reached out and took hold of Juliette's hand. But only for a moment before he turned and walked away from the bed, and Ivelis let go of Damien's hand and followed him.

And neither Marco nor Ivelis spoke during dinner. Or afterward, when they did their drawing assignment for school. Or later, when they went to bed.

But Damien didn't speak either as, for the

first time in his life, he felt overwhelmed. Too overwhelmed to function. Too overwhelmed to speak. Too overwhelmed to make sense of anything. Except this. Seeing Marco's little hand in Juliette's—this was what Damien wanted. All of it. The whole picture. Everything he'd never wanted before. And everything he so badly wanted now, yet still wouldn't admit, for fear he couldn't have it.

"Where is she?" the booming voice demanded from outside, on the doorstep.

Damien, who was just then exiting the clinic, spun around to the door to face the man. "Who?" Actually, he did know. Who else would have trekked out into the middle of godforsaken nowhere in crisply pressed khaki pants and a blue cotton dress shirt to find Juliette, other than her father? Asking Padre Benicio to go to Cima de la Montaña to contact the man was one thing, but standing here now and facing him—it put fear in him. A new fear. A different fear. The fear that he would take Juliette back with him. That he would never see her again.

"My daughter, Juliette. Tell me this is the place,

because I've had a hell of a time getting out here, and I hope I don't have to continue searching for her."

"She's here," Damien conceded, pointing to the open ward behind him. "First bed on the right."

"I don't understand," Alexander Allen said, still keeping his distance from the door. "What was she doing here? I'd been led to believe she was working for a company in San José, so how the hell did she end up here, with malaria?"

"How she ended up here is that she answered my ad. I needed another doctor to help me in the hospital, and Juliette was the one who came out here to do that. As for the malaria—this is Central America. People here get bitten by mosquitoes. Mosquitoes carry the parasite and Juliette was one of the unfortunate ones who had a vaccination against it that didn't work. Look, she's sleeping right now. In fact, she's slept for the past several days. A fitful sleep, sometimes so close to the verge of consciousness you think that she's simply going to open her eyes and smile as if nothing was wrong. So she might wake up if she hears your voice. Come in and talk to her." God knew he'd been talking, and talking, and getting nothing back from her.

"Has she been conscious at all, from the start of this?" Alexander asked.

"Briefly. I explained what was happening to her and how I was treating her, and I guess that's all she needed to hear because she went back to sleep and hasn't woken up since."

"What's her prognosis?" Alexander asked, sounding very stiff about it.

"Physically, she's stable."

"Her vitals are maintaining?"

"Pretty much. No major problems."

He nodded, as if taking it all under consideration. "And prior to her collapse, she was showing no symptoms?"

"She was tired, but around here we all get tired, so it didn't seem unusual."

"But you continued to allow her to work, even though you knew she was tired." Stated, not asked.

"That's just one of the facts of life in this hospital. We always work under difficult circumstances. Juliette knew that before she accepted the position, and she was good with it."

"Why this hospital, though? That's what I don't understand. She chose to work here when she could have had her choice of any proper medical institution in the world. So, what is it I'm not seeing?"

He wasn't seeing Juliette. Not at all. But Damien wasn't going to step into that mess. It wasn't his place. So, instead, he ignored the question, as it was Juliette's father's to answer.

"Juliette was sleeping lighter than she has been when I looked in on her a few minutes ago, so go on in and..."

"You're not worried that she's still unconscious?" Alexander interrupted.

"Worried as hell." Beyond worried. But that was something Alexander Allen didn't have to know. "But she's getting the correct medication, and we're taking good care of her, and waiting—which is all we can do."

"I want her transferred to another hospital. To *my* hospital."

"Against medical advice, Doctor. Juliette's in no condition to travel anywhere."

"With all due respect, she's not in any condition to stay here, either. In case you haven't noticed, her illness is not manifesting itself in the normal way, which means something, or someone, is going wrong. My intention with this, Doctor, is to save my daughter's life, *not* to spare your feelings."

The thin thread of civility between them was nearing its snapping point. And Damien was nearing his own snapping point. With the exception of the past few minutes, he'd spent most of an entire shift sitting at Juliette's bedside, holding her hand, wondering if someone else could do better by her. Wondering if, somehow, he'd gone wrong. Doubting himself. Doubting his decisions. And now, here was her father, practically throwing all Damien's doubts in his face. Accusing him of not being good enough, the way Nancy's father had done.

"Then we agree on something, since my intention is to save Juliette's life, and I don't give a damn about my feelings because they don't matter in this." His impassive facade was beginning to slip, and he wasn't sure what to do to put it back in place. Wasn't sure he even wanted to. Not for *this* man.

For the first time, Damien realized just why

Juliette had been so keen to get away from her father. And Alexander Allen's wealth had nothing whatsoever to do with Damien's mounting hostility toward him. Which, surprisingly, was a step in a completely different direction for him. It made Damien wonder if it was not the wealth he hated so much as the way some people acted because of it. That eye-opener gave him a whole new perspective of Juliette. Caused him to see something in her that he'd refused to see before. The fact was, she wasn't spoiled, as he'd first assumed. She wasn't caught up in the trappings of wealth, but she was trying to escape the way her father was caught up in them. And he owed her an apology for that, and for all the other wrong assumptions he'd made. When she woke up—

"There's a chair next to Juliette's bed." One that was probably warm from all the hours he'd spent in it. "Please feel free to stay as long as you wish. We don't have visiting hours here. Oh, and if you'd like something to eat or drink, just ask. I'll be in and out for a while, as will my nurse, Alegria, and a couple of our volunteers."

With that, Damien turned and walked back into the empty clinic, and shut the door behind him, then slumped against it. He was so sick with worry over Juliette he could barely function, and part of him wanted her father to take her back home with him to get her other help. But part of him feared that once she was gone from Bombacopsis, he'd never see her again. That was the part he feared most. Because he loved Juliette. Pure and simple. He'd gone and done the thing he'd promised himself he wouldn't do and he was about to lose her, without ever having told her how he felt. That was the worst part—he'd never told her.

CHAPTER TEN

"YOUR FATHER WAS here today, Juliette. Did you hear him?" It was dark now, and Bombacopsis was staying away from the hospital. No minor complaints coming across the threshold, no major complaints in queue. They were staying away out of respect, and Damien appreciated that as he didn't want to leave Juliette's side. He also didn't have it in him to do any doctoring. Something about seeing Juliette lying there, so pale, so helpless—slipping away from him. "He's staying with one of the families in the village tonight, even though I don't think he's happy about the arrangement. But it was the best we could do for him.

"The hospital's quiet, too. No patients at the moment. Oh, and you'll be happy to hear that there are no other cases of malaria in the village. We asked people to come in to be checked, and George went out door-to-door the other day, and we're all good. So when you wake up and get back to work…" Wake up? Back to work? The words were so painful to say, he almost choked on them. "When you wake up and get back to work you won't have to be treating a crisis." Damien raised his hand to his forehead and rubbed the spot just above his nose, directly between his eyes, the spot where a relentless throb had set in and wouldn't let go. She'd been like this a week now and he felt so helpless. So damned helpless.

"Marco and Ivelis are fine. They've been in to see you every day, and Marco is actually beginning to talk a little bit. Not Ivelis, though, although sometimes I think she's right on the verge. Padre Benicio is keeping them up with their schooling, and he says they're both very bright. Apparently, Marco is good with numbers. Oh, and Ivelis—she's a budding artist. Draws lovely pictures. Anyway, they're staying with George and Carmelita until you get better. It's a little crowded but, with help from so many of the locals, it's working out. Everybody in Bombacopsis is concerned about you, Juliette."

Small talk. It was all just small talk, and he

felt awkward about it because he wanted to tell her that he loved her. But he wanted her to hear it. Wanted to see her reaction when he said the words. Wanted her to laugh at him, or fight him, or kiss him. Wanted to look into her eyes to see if they reflected any love for him.

"Your dad's a formidable man, but you already know that, don't you. I hope you don't mind that I had him called to come see you. But I thought he needed to be here. Also, just in case you don't know where you are when you wake up, it's probably going to be back in Indianapolis. Your dad is making arrangements to have you transported there. He doesn't think we're doing enough for you here."

Damien took hold of Juliette's hand, and kissed the back of it. And he fought back the lump in his throat that was threatening to explode, because Juliette needed him to be strong right now. Strong enough for the both of them. "And I don't want you to go, Juliette. I don't ever want you to go. Which is why I need for you to wake up and tell me what *you* want. If you do that, sweetheart, I'll fight for it with everything I am. I promise."

"You don't have the right to keep her here," the voice from behind him said.

Damien twisted to see Alexander Allen looming over the foot of his daughter's bed. "But do you have the right to take her back to a place she doesn't want to go?"

"Legally, yes I do."

"What about morally? Have you ever, once, done anything for Juliette that she wanted, and not what you wanted for her?" He didn't want to have this argument with the man. Especially not with Juliette here. Whether or not she could hear, he didn't know. But he wanted to believe she could. Wanted to believe that his words were getting through to her on some level and making a difference. "Have you ever listened to her, Dr. Allen?"

"My whole life. And even though you think I'm being an ogre, all I want to do is what I believe is right for my daughter."

"What's right for Juliette is to wait until she wakes up to make the decisions herself."

"And in the meantime?"

"We talk to her and give her a reason to want to come back to us."

"That's not exactly a medical cure, is it?" Alexander Allen said. But his voice wasn't stern. Now, it was full of worry, and fear. The voice of a loving father.

"When she found out her vaccination hadn't worked, she was afraid the antimalarials we might give her wouldn't work, either. And I promised her they would." And she'd trusted him. Damn it, she'd trusted him!

"You had no way of knowing."

"But I shouldn't have promised."

"I'm sure my daughter needed to hear that promise from you." He stepped up to the bed and squeezed Damien's shoulder. "Look, son. I know you care for her. I think you might even be in love with her. But right now, I want to take her home. I've got an expert there—he's expecting her."

"Her body is weak, Dr. Allen. She's been unconscious for quite a while now and her overall condition may be stable, but the physical strain of putting her through what it would take to get her transported may be more than she's able to withstand." That, and the fact that he simply wanted her here. Wanted to be the one to take care of her. "In the end, I just want to do what's best for Juliette, and I think staying here's what's best."

"We both want what's best for Juliette, Dr. Caldwell. In my medical opinion, she's fit to travel. So, tomorrow morning, I'm returning to San José to arrange for an ambulance to come get her, and I'm also going to hire air transport to get us back to Indianapolis. If all goes as I hope it will, Juliette and I will be leaving the day after tomorrow. So spend your time with her now. Say what you have to say to her. I won't interrupt that. But do know that I'm taking her home with me, and I'm not going to be persuaded to change my mind."

Damien didn't respond to that. How could he? What was there to say?

"Remember when you first came here," Damien said to Juliette a little while later, after her father had gone. "And you promised that someday, someway, you were going to challenge me, and I wouldn't see it coming? Well, this is the challenge, Juliette. But I did see it coming when I sent for your father. I knew what he would do. The thing is, I think I know what you'd do, too.

And you're going to have to wake up and do it, because I can't do it for you. Do you hear me, Juliette? Squeeze my hand if you hear me."

But she didn't squeeze his hand, and he was crushed. "OK, if you can't squeeze my hand, can you wiggle your toes, or open your eyes? Anything to give me a sign?" Yet still no sign, and he was crushed again. Maybe later—

Damien stretched his shoulders and rolled his neck to fight back the stiffness settling into his muscles, then he took a drink of water from the cup sitting on the bedside stand, and exhaled a deep breath. Bent down, kissed Juliette on the forehead, then tenderly, fully on her lips. "Did I ever tell you about the time my brother Daniel and I burned down the next door neighbor's shed?"

And so it went into the night. Damien talked until he was hoarse, while Juliette slept.

"You look terrible."

Damien bolted up in his chair, blinked open his eyes and looked around. He must have dozed off for a moment. And now he was a little off on his orientation. It was daylight, but barely. He'd been sleeping for—what? Maybe two hours. Then something—a voice? Had someone spoken to him? Was that what had startled him out of his sleep? Or was he dreaming it?

It sounded like Juliette but, looking over at her, he saw that her eyes were still closed.

"Morning, Juliette," he said, standing up to stretch his body. He looked a mess. His hair was in disarray. His scrubs wrinkled beyond recognition. His normal three-day stubble gone way beyond that. He needed to grab a shower, wash his hair, shave, put on some fresh clothes, grab a bite to eat since he couldn't remember the last time he'd been anywhere near a plate of food. Yes, he had a long list of things he needed to do, but hated to do, as they would take him away from Juliette longer than he wanted.

Damien bent down, kissed her on the forehead and took hold of her hand. "Juliette," he said, "I've got to go make myself presentable. But I won't be gone long. I promise. And while I'm gone, I'm going to have Alegria come in and bathe you, and change your linens—just so you'll know what's going on around you. Also, it's Friday morning, and you've been sleeping for eight days now."

He'd oriented her first thing every morning, but he'd never, ever used the words *coma* or *unconscious. Asleep* sounded much more gentle—much more hopeful. And he needed some hope here. Desperately needed some hope.

Before he left Juliette, Damien pushed his chair back to the wall, then took a look out the window directly over Juliette's bed. It was beautiful out today. Sunny. Cheery. For a moment he thought about carrying Juliette outside, to let some of that sun sink into her body. Maybe she would feel its warmth. Maybe she would taste the difference between the stale hospital air and the fresh air out there. Of course, it was only a thought. A rather silly one at that. Fresh air and sunlight didn't cure malaria or, in Juliette's case, the toxic side effects of the drug used to treat malaria.

Bending down to kiss her once more before he left, he pushed the hair back from her face. "This won't take me long," he said, then turned away from the bed and headed to the opening between the two partitions set at the end of it.

"Could she comb my hair?"

Damien spun to face Juliette. But her eyes weren't open. "I'll ask her," he said cautiously, even though his heart was about to leap out of his chest. "Anything else you want?"

The reply came, but it seemed to take forever. "Water," she said eventually. "Dry throat."

Damien bit down hard on his lower lip, trying to control his emotions. "A few sips. It's been a while since you've had anything in your stomach, and I don't want you cramping up."

"I'm a doctor." Finally, she opened her eyes. "I know that."

"Juliette…" Damien choked out, stumbling back to her bedside and pulling her up into his arms. "We were so afraid… I was so afraid…" He moved back away from her. "Do you know how long you've been out?"

"You've been reminding me every day."

"You've heard me?"

She let out a weary sigh, and nodded. "I heard you sometimes." Then she closed her eyes and snuggled her head against his arm. "And like I said a few minutes ago, you look terrible."

She held out her hand to his, and he took hold. "Don't leave me yet, Damien. Please, just sit with me for a while."

"For as long as you want," he said, bending down to kiss her hand. "For as long as you want."

"You *know* my dad wasn't too happy about my staying here," Juliette said. She was sitting outside in the sun today, three days after she'd awoken, and she was greeting the many visitors who'd casually dropped by to say hello, bring her flowers or simply hang around hoping to help her out in any way they could. She was truly touched by the sentiment, and shocked to discover how highly regarded she was in Bombacopsis.

Damien, who'd pulled out a chair next to her, and was taking in the sun as well, smiled lazily. "He'll get over it."

"I'm glad he was here, though."

"I was afraid you'd hate me for sending for him."

Juliette laughed. "No. He needed to be here. It would have hurt him if you hadn't sent for him, and I really don't want him hurt. He loves me, Damien. And maybe he's a little too overprotective, but that's just the way he is."

"I know your dad means well, Juliette. I think he'd move heaven and earth to take care of you.

And while we didn't necessarily agree on what was best for you, I think he's a good man."

"He *is* a good man," she agreed. "And a good doctor." She was touched by Damien's kind words, especially since her father and Damien had been on opposite ends of the debate on how to best take care of her.

"Well, all I know is, we both agreed that we wanted what was best for you, even though we wanted it done differently."

"Wouldn't it have been easier on you to let me go back with him?"

"No," he said quite simply. "I wanted you here."

But why did he want her here? Why wouldn't he just say the words? She knew he loved her. There was no doubt in her mind. But she wanted him to tell her, and she was afraid he never would. Yet she'd felt his kisses when she was somewhere smothered deep in her fog. Felt his hand holding hers. Heard the words, but never the right words. The words that would have soothed her heart.

"Well, it's a good thing I woke up and made the decision for myself."

"But staying in Costa Rica is going to be very

difficult for you, especially now that you don't have a job here."

"Can you believe they'd do that to me?" she asked, sounding more angry than hurt.

"I don't think it was nice of them, but I can believe it. People look after their own best interests, and your employers needed to move on at a time when you couldn't. Would I have done that to you? No, I believe in loyalty. But you were apparently working for someone who didn't." Her company had laid her off days ago, after he'd sent Padre Benicio to call Cynthia and ask her to explain Juliette's absence to her employer. The director of her office had sent an impersonal note explaining his circumstances and said, if Juliette recovered sufficiently, she could reapply should another position come open. But, as he'd explained, he had too many medical professionals waiting in queue, and they had to be attended to immediately.

"Well, it stings. And more than that, it leaves me stranded here needing to find work or else I'll be forced to leave in ninety days, thanks to the visa requirements."

"And ninety days to find work may be unrealistic, considering that you'll still be recovering from your malaria and the hospitals here might not be so eager to take you on due to your medical situation. But maybe going home is what you need to do, considering how badly you responded to standard malaria treatment."

It almost sounded as if he wanted her to leave. Between losing her job, and now this…

"There are other cures, Damien. A whole host of other drugs I can try. And I still have the hospital here, if you'll let me work." Would he let her, though? Over the past couple of days, she'd given it a lot of thought then reconciled herself to the fact that here, with Damien, at this little hospital, was where she was happiest. What she didn't know, however, was if her being here made him happy. But since the rest of her world seemed to be crumbling at her feet right now, it seemed like the perfect time to find out if this little piece of it was, too.

"Will you let me stay and work for you?"

"But how would you support yourself since I can't pay you?" he asked.

This wasn't what she wanted to hear. No, what she wanted to hear was him telling her how thrilled he'd be to have her stay, that he wanted it more than anything. That they could have a bright future together here. He hadn't said any of that, though. Hadn't even sounded close to anything hopeful. "Remember—I'm rich. I don't need for you to pay me."

"Could you actually work under these conditions, Juliette? I know you can do it for a couple days a week, but do you even realize what it's going to be like if you're here every day, all day? And there's no phone connection. No internet—"

And again, nothing hopeful. "I'm well aware of what you don't have here, Damien." This hurt. When she'd thought he loved her—had she mistaken that for something else? Something she didn't understand? Had she truly believed everything had changed between them when nothing had? Nothing at all?

Suddenly, Juliette felt tired. Overwhelmed. Sad. Didn't want to sit outside anymore. Didn't want to talk to Damien. Didn't even want to see him. Wanted to get away from him before the tears came. "I need to go back to my bed and rest," she said, scooting forward in her chair, ready to stand up.

Damien sprang immediately to his feet to help her, but she held out her hand to stop him. “I’m fine,” she snapped. “I can do this by myself.”

“You’ve only been awake three days, Juliette, and you’re still weak.” In spite of her protests, he stepped forward to take her arm. But she shook him off.

“I *said*, I can do this by myself.” Brave words, even though her legs were still weak, and her back still ached from too much time flat in bed.

“Damn it, Juliette! What the hell’s wrong?”

“Wrong? Do you want to know what’s wrong, Damien? You’re what’s wrong. And I’m what’s wrong.”

“Why are we fighting?”

“Because that’s what we do. We have since the first day I stepped into the hospital, and while I’d thought we’d gotten past that, apparently I was wrong.” She took two steps toward the front entry to the hospital and her legs gave out on her, causing her to lurch forward. But Damien was there to catch her before she fell, and for a moment she clung to him, wishing that his desire to hold her came from something more than simply trying to keep her from hurting herself.

"Juliette, I—" he started, his voice almost in a whisper.

Why didn't he just tell her that he loved her? That would make everything right. But he was running out of chances, and she was running out of hope. Whatever was holding him back was still hanging on, and she didn't know how to break through it. Not even her near-death had broken through it.

"Look, Damien. I can't get out of here on my own yet, but I've decided to talk to Padre Benicio, to see if he can find someone to help me get back to San José. I'll have my dad help me from there. I think that's best for everybody concerned." For everybody but her. But falling in love with a man who kept himself hidden from love was impossible to deal with. She wasn't strong enough, now. Her defenses were gone. And, for the first time in her life, she found herself totally without direction.

It was time to go home.

"I think you should stay here for a while. The children need you—"

The children, but not Damien. "The children will be fine. They've got you, and you're turning into a great dad." She did hate to leave Marco and Ivelis. In fact, the idea that she'd never see them again was tearing her apart. It was amazing how quickly she'd come to love them. But they were great kids. So full of life and eagerness. So adaptable to their new situation. So easy to love. Juliette's throat tightened when she thought about walking away from them, but she couldn't allow the emotions she knew would come from that sad scene to stop her from doing what she had to do. The children would get along without her and, as much as Damien loved them, he would eventually adopt them. Maybe he didn't know that yet, but she did.

"But they huddle around you every minute they can."

Juliette smiled. "And they adore you, Damien. The thing is, I can't stay here only because the children need me, especially when I know they've got a wonderful life ahead of them."

"I want to keep them, Juliette, but I don't know how. They need more than I can provide them."

"Do you love them?" she asked.

He nodded. "It snuck up on me, but yes, I do."

He could admit his love for the children, but not

for her. It hurt. "Then that's all they need. The rest will work itself out. See, you *need* to be a father, Damien. And once you realize that, you're going to discover some happiness you never thought you could have." But what he wouldn't realize was that he needed to be a husband. It was too late for that now, and she had to leave before her emotions affected the children. "Look, I won't be going for a couple days, because I'm not up to the travel yet, so I'll have plenty of time to say my proper goodbyes to Marco and Ivelis. And I'll be gentle about it, Damien, because I don't want to hurt them."

"You won't be coming back again, will you?"

His face was shielded from her, but she wanted to think it was covered with sadness.

"I think it's time for you to run your ad again. Now, if you'll help me back to bed, I really do need to rest." And fight back the tears that wanted to flow. And pray that her heart wouldn't hurt any more than it did at this moment.

Damien looked at the truck parked outside the hospital's front entrance, then turned his head away. He didn't want to see it, didn't want it to be here. But it was, and there was no denying the fact that Juliette was about to climb into that truck and leave his life for good. He'd struggled with this for two days now. Struggled from the moment she'd told him she was going until this very second. Why was he letting her do this? Why wasn't he trying to stop her?

Because she deserved better than this. And *this*, he was coming to realize, was where he was going to stay because, for the first time in his life, he fit. Anyplace else, he floundered. Either way, it wasn't enough to offer her.

Did he want her to stay? More than anything. Did he want to work with her and love her and marry her and raise an army of kids with her? He did, so much so that when he thought about life without her he couldn't breathe. Yet he couldn't ask. Didn't have that right because he knew that to have Juliette here would be to deprive her of a life where she truly belonged. Yes, she was a rich girl. And yes, she was used to privilege. But she wasn't spoiled by it. He'd been so wrong about that. So terribly wrong. But it was a wrong he couldn't right because, if he did, she would fall into his arms and tell him how much she loved him and if she did that he'd never be able to let her go. And, for Juliette's sake, she had to go.

"You know you're going to have to do something about this, don't you?" George said. He was standing in the clinic door, watching Damien purposely turn his back to the hospital entrance.

"About what?" he said, even though he knew exactly what.

"How stupid can any one man be, Damien? You love her, she loves you—admit it to yourself, you damned fool, then admit it to her, and the rest will be easy."

"Easy?" Damien spun to face the man. "This isn't easy, George. And it can't be easy, no matter what I do. Juliette belongs in a different world, and in time she'll remember that. Then she'll resent me for telling her that I love her because that's what would hold her here. And I don't have the right to hold her because all I'll ever be able to give her is a run-down, underfunded little hospital and a hut with maybe enough room to add another room or two."

"The village will build you a proper house, Damien, if that's what's concerning you."

"Hell, they can build me a mansion. But that's still not good enough."

"What's 'good enough,' Damien, is what she wants. Have you ever asked her what she wants?"

Damien turned to look out the front door. The damned truck was still there, still waiting. Still breaking his heart. "Nobody has," he whispered. "Not her father. Not me."

"You're right," Juliette said, exiting the hospital ward. "Nobody has."

George walked over to Damien, squeezed him on the shoulder, then retreated back into the clinic and closed the door.

"Why is that, Damien?" Juliette asked. "Why didn't you ask me?"

"Because I was afraid you'd tell me."

"Do you really not want me here that much?" she asked.

"No. I really *do* want you here that much." This was, perhaps, the most honest thing he'd ever said to her. Maybe the most honest thing he'd ever said to anyone.

Juliette stepped up to him, her face to his back, but maintained a few inches of separation between them. "Then ask me, Damien. Ask me what I want."

He wanted to, but did he really have that right? "If I ask you, then what?"

"Then I'll know that, for the first time in my life, someone values me for who I am and not for who they want me to be."

Damien swallowed hard, then turned to face her. She was so close to him he could smell the scent of her shampoo—the shampoo she always brought with her for her weekends at Bombacopsis. The shampoo he'd grown to love. "What do you want, Juliette?" The most difficult words he'd ever uttered.

"I want to stay here, work in a little hospital where daily hardship is normal. Where I'll have to scrape for drugs and bandages. Where I'll have to make beds. And love a man who spends too much time worrying about the things he can't give me to fully understand what he *can* give me. Raise two lovely children who need both a mother and a father, and maybe add a couple more to the mix. Live in a hut, or a cottage, or a mansion or anywhere the man I love lives."

"And give up everything you've ever known?"

"Yet have so much more than I ever expected to have. See, Damien. The thing about falling in love is, it changes everything. Several weeks ago, when I first came here, I wasn't sure I wanted to stay. And, to be honest, I had to do some pretty stern talking to myself to get me back here that second weekend. I loved the work, but I wasn't particularly anxious to work with you. But, you know, falling in love replaced all that. It changed me so much that by the third week I was actually looking forward to seeing you. I'd spent my whole week away from you wanting to see you. And it wasn't only you. I wanted to be part of the work here. It made me feel vital, and necessary. Back in Indianapolis, I was…replaceable. Any number of people could have stepped into my job at a moment's notice, and my absence there would have never been noticed. But here—it's the first time I've ever been necessary for who I was and not for who my father was, or who he wanted me to be. Being necessary—that's the highest calling a doctor can have. And you know what, it doesn't matter that I can't just send someone down the hall for a CT scan or an endoscopy, and all I may have available to fix a serious gash is a simple stick-on bandage. What matters—the *only* thing that matters—is that you and your hospital allow me to be the doctor I always knew I could be." She reached up and stroked his cheek. "What I want, Damien, is the rest of my life with you, but I'm not sure you want the rest of your life with me."

"Do you know what you're saying, Juliette? Do you understand what a life with me will be like?"

"It'll be difficult. It will lack the advantages I'm used to. It will be nothing that I'd ever planned for myself. And it will be wonderful because I'll be facing the challenges alongside the man I love, if the man I love loves me enough to want me there." She looked deep into his eyes to see if the answer showed, and what she saw was a softening she'd never seen before. Tenderness. Love.

"The man you love does love you. But he's terrified that the life he's offering you won't be good enough. That, in time, you'll grow to resent it, and him." He sighed deeply, lamentably. "And I couldn't bear that, Juliette. Knowing that I couldn't give you enough to make you happy—"

"Damien, I know what will make me happy. For the first time, I truly know. And it's not going to change because all I want from you is to have you love me."

"Juliette, I do love you. More than I can express. But I can't give you…Egyptian cotton bedsheets. In fact, I'll be damned lucky to give you a proper bed."

"Do you think I really care about Egyptian sheets, or proper beds? I'm not that shallow, Damien. Are you still hung up by my wealth?"

"I know you're not shallow, and I got over my rich girl lunacy shortly after I met you. But to love you is to *want* to give you everything. That coming from a man who has nothing."

"A man who has nothing? How can you say that, Damien?"

"Because it's true."

"What's true is that, to me, *everything* is waking up every morning and seeing the man I love lying there next to me. *Everything* is raising two wonderful children with the man I love and someday giving him another couple. *Everything* is working by his side, fighting the odds with him and knowing that, together, we can't be beaten. *Everything* is who you are to me, Damien. Don't you understand that? *You* are everything."

"Juliette, I… I…" Words failed him, but his actions didn't as he lowered his face to Juliette's, and sealed their unspoken vow with a deep, eternal kiss. A kiss that Juliette melted into and knew that there she would find the rest of her life.

Damien and Daniel Caldwell looked the handsome pair, standing outside the village church in their matching suits and matching ties, mixing and mingling with the few remaining wedding guests. If it weren't for the fact that Damien's hair was long and his face scruffy with stubble, a look she adored on him, and Daniel was clean-shaven with short hair, they were absolutely as identical as Damien had told her they were. Same bright eyes, same dimples to die for, same smile. Zoey, her new sister-in-law, was a lucky woman to have Daniel, and Juliette was a lucky woman to have Damien.

Juliette looked out into the garden, where Marco and Ivelis were playing with their soon-to-be new cousin, Maddie—Daniel and Zoey's daughter—and Diego, who'd seemed to latch on to their lives and wouldn't let go. Marco's and Ivelis's adoption wouldn't be final for a while, but they were already a family, in spite of the children's legal status. And what an amazing family it was—a joining of what, at times, seemed almost insurmountable odds.

"You know this means you're a grandfather now, don't you?" she said to her dad.

Alexander Allen cleared his throat, straightened up rigidly. "I'm too young to be a grandfather," he said, trying to sound stern. But there was no real sternness there. Not from the man who'd packed an entire suitcase full of toys for his new grandchildren.

"Well, Grandpa, like it or not, that's who you are now. And, for the next two weeks, you're going to have an awful lot of time to perfect it." When her father assumed temporary medical duties at the hospital and also took over the care of Marco and Ivelis, while she and Damien slipped away to Hawaii for a honeymoon.

"I did tell you that I'm having a few supplies delivered here because I refuse to work under such primitive conditions. Oh, and antimalarials. I'm having every kind on the market shipped down here so you'll have them on hand, since you insist on living here with the mosquitoes."

"Bring in whatever makes you comfortable, because Damien and I expect you to come visit us several times a year, and when you're here you know you *are* going to be expected to work with us."

Alexander finally conceded a laugh. "I was right, you know. I always did say you'd be a great administrator. Just didn't expect it to be in—" he spread his arms wide to gesture the entire village "—this!"

"Well, get used to *this*, because it's now your home away from home. In the meantime, the village is throwing us a festival and Damien and I need to put in an appearance."

"Only an appearance?" Alexander questioned.

"Only an appearance," Damien confirmed. "They tend to overindulge a little during their festivals around here, and Juliette and I need to go back to the hospital and get ready to take care of about half the villagers who'll eventually come in sometime later on." He took hold of his wife's hand, then leaned down and kissed her on the cheek. "It's just one of the things we do around here."

"Mind if I join you?" Alexander asked. "My

doctoring skills may be a little rusty but, since you really don't have anything to treat people with, I don't suppose anybody will notice."

"I'm in, too, bro," Daniel said, stepping into the mix with his wife. "And I'm serious about what I said. Zoey and I will be down here a couple times a year to help you out in the hospital."

"So I might as well get started tonight, too," Zoey said cheerfully. "If you could use a nurse on duty."

"We can always use a nurse on duty," Damien said.

In the distance, Juliette heard the sounds of the festival and smiled. This was going to be a great life. "Well, why don't you three head on over to the hospital, while Damien and I arrange for Padre Benicio to look after our children tonight, and we'll join you shortly. Oh, and scrubs are in the storage closet."

As Daniel, Zoey and Alexander set off together, Damien and Juliette stood in the road and watched after them for a bit. "This is good, Damien," Juliette said, turning to face him, and raising her arms to twist around his neck.

"Very good," he agreed, tilting her face up to his. "Very, *very* good."

And there, in the middle of the road, in a remote jungle village in the middle of Costa Rica, to the sound of revelers celebrating her marriage to Damien, Juliette kissed her husband with the first of a long lifetime of soul-shaking kisses. For the first time in her life, Juliette truly knew where she was meant to be.

* * * * *

If you enjoyed this story, check out these other great reads from Dianne Drake

THE NURSE AND THE SINGLE DAD
DOCTOR, MUMMY...WIFE?
TORTURED BY HER TOUCH
A HOME FOR THE HOT-SHOT DOC

All available now!

MILLS & BOON®

Large Print – January 2018

ROMANCE

The Tycoon's Outrageous Proposal	Miranda Lee
Cipriani's Innocent Captive	Cathy Williams
Claiming His One-Night Baby	Michelle Smart
At the Ruthless Billionaire's Command	Carole Mortimer
Engaged for Her Enemy's Heir	Kate Hewitt
His Drakon Runaway Bride	Tara Pammi
The Throne He Must Take	Chantelle Shaw
A Proposal from the Crown Prince	Jessica Gilmore
Sarah and the Secret Sheikh	Michelle Douglas
Conveniently Engaged to the Boss	Ellie Darkins
Her New York Billionaire	Andrea Bolter

HISTORICAL

The Major Meets His Match	Annie Burrows
Pursued for the Viscount's Vengeance	Sarah Mallory
A Convenient Bride for the Soldier	Christine Merrill
Redeeming the Rogue Knight	Elisabeth Hobbes
Secret Lessons with the Rake	Julia Justiss

MEDICAL

The Surrogate's Unexpected Miracle	Alison Roberts
Convenient Marriage, Surprise Twins	Amy Ruttan
The Doctor's Secret Son	Janice Lynn
Reforming the Playboy	Karin Baine
Their Double Baby Gift	Louisa Heaton
Saving Baby Amy	Annie Claydon

1217 GEN STD LP